DECORATED TO DEATH

Decorated to Death

Peg Marberg

WHEELER
CHIVERS

This Large Print edition is published by Wheeler Publishing, Waterville, Maine, USA and by BBC Audiobooks Ltd, Bath, England.
Wheeler Publishing, a part of Gale, Cengage Learning.
Copyright © 2008 by Peg Marberg.
The moral right of the author has been asserted.
An Interior Design Mystery.

The text of this Large Print edition is unabridged.
Other aspects of the book may vary from the original edition.
Set in 16 pt. Plantin.
Printed on permanent paper.

LIBRARY OF CONGRESS CATALOGING-IN-PUBLICATION DATA

Marberg, Peg.
  Decorated to death / by Peg Marberg.
    p. cm. — (An interior design mystery) (Wheeler Publishing large print cozy mystery)
  ISBN-13: 978-1-59722-776-6 (softcover : alk. paper)
  ISBN-10: 1-59722-776-5 (softcover : alk. paper)
    1. Interior decorators — Fiction. 2. Interior decoration — Fiction. 3. Indiana — Fiction. 4. Large type books. I. Title.
  PS3613.A728D43 2008
  813'.6—dc22   2008012119

BRITISH LIBRARY CATALOGUING-IN-PUBLICATION DATA AVAILABLE

Published in 2008 in the U.S. by arrangement with The Berkley Publishing Group, a member of Penguin Group (USA) Inc.
Published in 2008 in the U.K. by arrangement with The Berkley Publishing Group, a member of Penguin Group (USA) Inc.

U.K. Hardcover: 978 1 408 41219 0 (Chivers Large Print)
U.K. Softcover: 978 1 408 41220 6 (Camden Large Print)

Printed in the United States of America
1 2 3 4 5 6 7 12 11 10 09 08

To my family and in particular to Rich, Matt, Amanda, Steve, and Kevin. Bright young adults with bright futures.

ACKNOWLEDGMENTS

I wish to thank my husband, Ed, whose patience and understanding helped me throughout the writing of this book. I also wish to thank Sandra Harding, my editor, who also helped guide me through the process. I couldn't have done it without them.

CITIZENS OF
SEVILLE, INDIANA

Jean Hastings Interior designer and amateur sleuth

Charlie Hastings Jean's husband and retired investment counselor

JR Cusak The Hastingses' married daughter and Jean's business partner

Matt Cusak JR's husband and police lieutenant

Kerry and Kelly Cusak JR and Matt's children

Mary England Charlie's twin sister and Jean's best friend

Denny England Mary's husband and owner of England's Fine Furniture

Rollie Stevens Seville's chief of police

Martha Stevens Rollie's wife

Sally Birdwell Widow and Jean's neighbor

Billy Birdwell Sally's son and budding caterer

Tammie Flowers Billy's coworker and girlfriend

9

Amanda Little Real estate agent

Sid Rosen, Patti Crump, Jasper Merkle Seville police officers

Abner Wilson Elderly handyman

Stanley Wilson Abner's grandnephew and helper

Hilly R. Murrow News reporter

Horatio Bordeaux Entrepreneur and Jean's friend

Dr. Sue Lin Loo Medical examiner

VISITORS TO SEVILLE, INDIANA

Dr. Peter Parker Physician, surgeon, and nephew of vacationing Doc Parker

Dona Deville Diet diva

Rufus (Ruffy) Halsted Real estate tycoon wannabe and Dona's ex

Ellie Halsted Dona and Ruffy's daughter

Vincent Salerno Ellie's bodyguard

Todd Masters Employee of Dona Deville

Marsha (Goody) Gooding Dona's personal assistant

Maxine Roberts Dona's public relations person

CHAPTER ONE

It was a perfect midsummer day in America's heartland. For a change, the local weather forecast included neither the threat of an afternoon shower nor the prospect of an extended heat wave. In the backyard of my Seville, Indiana, home (located in the central part of the Hoosier state), I was enjoying a second cup of morning coffee. The house, an English-style cottage, was built in the late 1940s by Archibald Kettle, a dedicated Anglophile, who dubbed his creation Kettle Cottage, a name that stuck. Some thirty-plus years ago, my husband, Charles William Hastings, presented me with the keys to the place. I, in turn, presented Charlie with Jean Junior (aka JR), our first and only child.

From the flagstone patio, ensconced in a green-cushioned white wicker chair, I watched as a charm of finches, an immature cardinal, and a pair of white-breasted nuthatches hopped about in the leafy branches of the redbud tree. The yard had never looked better, thanks to the efforts of my husband, a retired investment counselor. And thanks to his devotion to the game of golf, Charlie wasn't there to share the morning, or the moment, with me. Instead, the role of companion fell to Pesty, a pampered six-year-old Keeshond.

With eyes as black as her nose, the pudgy pooch stared wistfully at the cottage's back door. The warm, humid air had turned the little Kees's black and silvery coat into an unruly mound of fuzzy fur. She literally looked like a wolf in sheep's clothing. But, her "been there, done that" attitude indicated that Pesty was ready to trade the great outdoors for the great indoors. The opportunity to do so came when the shrill ring of the kitchen phone brought us both to our feet and into the house.

"Designer Jeans. Jean Hastings speaking. How may I help you?" I said, catching my breath. Somehow I had managed (sans reading glasses), to push the correct button on Charlie's latest Internet purchase — a skinny, Day-Glo pink, high-impact-plastic, wireless telephone. The monstrosity had more options than a Chinese dinner menu.

"And this is England's Fine Furniture

14

calling. Mary England speaking," Charlie's twin replied. Her voice overflowed with a natural exuberance. "How about having lunch at the club today?" she said, referring to the Sleepy Hollow Country Club. "Just you and me, Gin. No husbands, no kids, no grandkids, and no hassles. Or are you too busy?"

"I wish. Unfortunately, my work schedule is about as empty as Pesty's food dish. I think I'm paying the price for operating an interior design business in a town with a population of fewer than thirty thousand."

Designer Jeans came into being some twelve-plus years ago as a cure for my midlife crisis, which was initiated by an empty nest and exacerbated by Charlie's early retirement. According to JR, my junior partner, Designer Jeans is a viable business thanks to my brain and her brawn.

"I didn't go back to school, pass the National Council for Interior Design Qualification exam, and join the United Federation of Interior Designers just to end up competing with Abner Wilson and his grandnephew for jobs," I grumbled. "While I don't mind washing walls or even painting a few fences, I'm not all that keen on trash removal. Although, if you believe the latest gossip making its way around town, that end of the business has become a real money-maker for the old grouch."

"Well," said the perpetually cheerful Mary, "if things are as bad as you say for Designer Jeans, then I think you'll be especially interested in what I've got to tell you. You know, Gin, I believe this is your lucky day."

My friendship with Mary (an attractive, albeit overweight, blithe spirit) began when we were mere toddlers and has continued to this day. She is both my best friend and sister-in-law. Still, I was about to chide her for her continuous use of my childhood nickname when she nearly rendered me deaf with an ear-piercing scream.

"Oh my stars! Gin, I've got to go. Herbie's demonstrating a king-size sofa bed for a customer. The last time he did that, it took more than three hours to get him free. Even the firemen couldn't figure out how he got himself stuck in it. Noon at the club. Bye-bye."

The call ended, leaving me with some unanswered questions, none of which pertained to the furniture store's salesman, the ambiguous Herbie Waddlemeyer. What did Mary have to tell me? And why did she believe that it was my lucky day? Friday the thirteenth isn't exactly a stellar date on anybody's calendar, and certainly not on mine. My inherited Irish intuition kicked in, leaving me with an uneasy feeling.

The feeling increased as a murder of crows came into view. Breaking formation as they flew over the yard, the ominous black birds staged a noisy reunion in the nearby woods. Listening to the ruckus, I felt about as lucky as an overfed canary trapped in a room full of underfed felines.

"Hey, snap out of it," I said in a voice loud enough to wake the dead and the napping Pesty, "this is Indiana. Crows are like basketball hoops — they're everywhere. Leave the pondering and foreboding to Poe. You're an interior designer, not a master of mystery. Now, go get ready for lunch."

Maybe the dog didn't appreciate my little lecture, but it did me a lot of good. Mentally, I'd crossed over to the sunny side of the street, and I was determined to stay there, even if it killed me.

A huffing Pesty followed me up the oak staircase and into the master bedroom. Making herself comfortable in the middle of the crazy-quilt-covered four-poster bed, the sleepy Kees watched with drooping eyelids as I began searching the bedroom closet for a change of clothes. I'd decided to ditch the outfit that I had on (a coffee-stained, olive-drab camp shirt and shorts) for something more in keeping with my budding, cheerful disposition.

After considering everything from the ridiculous (a green chenille jumpsuit) to the sublime (ivory satin lounging pajamas), I chose my old, white linen pantsuit with its fickle zipper and my new teal camisole. The suit made the best of my less-than-perfect figure, and the camisole complemented the suit.

A quick shower and shampoo followed by a few passes with the hair dryer took care of my chin-length, gray-streaked auburn tresses. A fast application of peach blusher with matching lip gloss, a smidgen of shadow to bring out the blue in my gray eyes, and I was ready to wiggle into my clothes.

Checking my reflection in the hall mirror before leaving the house, I was pleased. For a tall, bony, senior citizen (a label today's society bestows on anyone ordering dinner from the special early-bird menu at a chain restaurant), I looked pretty spiffy, thanks to good health, genes, and my choice of outfits.

In retrospect, I was as wrong about the suit (the zipper on the pants split when I arrived at the club) as Mary was about it being my lucky day. Had I followed my Irish intuition, skipped lunch, and spent the remainder of the day in the bathtub with a stack of home decor magazines, there's no telling how differently things might have turned out.

CHAPTER TWO

The noonday sun distributed a myriad of rays across Sleepy Hollow's eighteen-hole golf course. Like sheep in a meadow, small clusters of golfers moved slowly across the rolling hills and narrow fairways.

Turning into the parking lot, I was pleasantly surprised to discover that the valet parking sign was displayed. From the number of golfers I'd observed on the course, I knew that the odds of my finding an empty parking place would be chancy at best. I handed the minivan's keys to the young, gum-chewing male attendant. Like Speed Racer, the kid moved fast and drove even faster. Shoving the parking receipt in my purse, I said a quick prayer for the safe return of my vehicle and walked boldly into the clubhouse, broken zipper be damned.

The Sleepy Hollow clubhouse was built in the 1920s and was originally designed as a gambling casino. After a short stint as a servicemen's club during the 1940s, the place was turned into a country club complete with an eighteen-hole golf course and full service clubhouse. Because of its white stucco exterior, orange-colored tile roof, and arched porticoes, the rambling structure belongs on a California hillside where kitsch isn't just appreciated, it's revered. Instead, the clubhouse, which some people claim resembles a hat box flanked by two steamer trunks, sits on a bluff on the outskirts of Seville, a small Indiana town founded in the 1870s by Garrison Seville, a Civil War hero. Personally, I like the way the old place looks both inside and out.

Last fall, Designer Jeans handled the redesign of the club's main dining room. Although the room wasn't open for lunch, I couldn't resist opening the frosted-glass double doors and taking a peek. The Art Deco decor that JR and I had reintroduced into the room looked as crisp and fresh as the day we had finished the project.

The overall color scheme of white, black, and red with gold accents was as elegant as it was chic. All the hours removing old wallpaper had paid off, as had the time I spent applying a faux marble finish to the walls. The huge black-lacquered sideboard with its black granite top was the room's fo-

21

cal point. I'd draped a richly embroidered fringe shawl across the cabinet's top and held it in place with a large, bronze sculptured elephant that I'd picked up for next to nothing at a flea market. Snowy white cloths topped the Gilbert Rohde reproduction dining sets. The chrome and leather chairs proved to be as durable and as comfortable as they looked. If I didn't know better, I'd swear that the three fake King palms I'd placed where the bar once stood had grown since last fall.

Walking back across the black-and-white ceramic tile floor, I gave the bronze pachyderm a parting pat on the rump for good luck and exited the room.

With my spirits buoyed by my visit to one of Designer Jeans' most successful projects, I headed down to the west corridor leading to the club's bar and grill, where lunch was being served and Mary was waiting for me.

Resplendent in a floral shift, Mary had been seated in the grill's oversized back booth. In the darkened recess of the adjacent bar area, Charlie and his brother-in-law, Denny England, Mary's husband and owner of England's Fine Furniture, were rehashing their golf match while wolfing down a quick lunch of hot dogs, onion rings, and beer. What was left of their attention span was taken up by the bar's new flat-screen, high-definition television set that, as usual, was tuned to the Golf Channel. Not wanting to compete with Tiger Woods, I bypassed the bar and headed straight for the grill's back booth and my destiny.

Knowing Mary as well as I do, I decided to eat first and ask questions later. Mary and I made short work of the French onion soup and grilled cheese sandwiches. Then, while Mary enjoyed a whipped-cream, double-fudge éclair dessert, I enjoyed a cup of coffee and a cigarette. My enjoyment lasted about as long as the éclair.

"My stars," said Mary, licking bits of the calorie-laden pastry from her fork, "you're the only one I know who still smokes. You know if you had used the patch when I did, you'd be smoke-free by now. Try it. Not only will your heart and lungs thank you, your taste buds will, too. I know mine did."

Obviously. Finished with the dessert and the pitch for the patch, Mary reached for her glass of sweet tea. Taking a dainty sip, she sat back and waited for the usual Jean Hastings sharp retort. What she received instead was a nod of my head and a thin smile. Granted, it wasn't much but given that I was still in the process of adjusting to this sunny side of life stuff, I felt it was more than enough. Judging from her reaction, I sensed that Mary disagreed.

"Are you all right? You're not sick, are you? Is there something you're not telling me? Oh my stars, is it life threatening? Does Charlie know? What can I do to help?"

"Jeez, Mar, knock it off. People are starting to stare. There is nothing, I repeat, nothing wrong with me. I was just being nice," I snarled. "It's part of my new, sunny persona, in case you haven't noticed."

"Oh, thank heavens, you really are all right. For a minute there, you scared me. You looked just like Herbie did when he was stuck in that sofa bed."

Only a fool fights on when the battle is lost. Signaling to Tammie, the curvaceous, ditzy waitress with reddish-blond hair, I ordered a second éclair for Mary and a refill on my coffee.

"Friends?" ventured Mary, plunging a fork into the small mountain of whipped cream. The fluffy white topping mimicked Mary's hairdo in texture, color, and design.

"Always," I assured her, raising my coffee cup in a salute to our long and solid friendship.

Once our addictions (chocolate and caffeine) had been sufficiently satisfied, it was time to get down to business.

"Okay, Mary, now tell me something I don't know. Why do you think it's my lucky day, and what does that have to do with Designer Jeans?"

"Well," said Mary, dabbing her cupid's bow mouth with a napkin and emitting a small burp, "remember two weeks ago when we had that big sale? The day Herbie caught his tie in the cash register?" Not waiting for an answer, Mary rushed on. "Thank goodness it was one of those clip-on things, otherwise he might have been seriously hurt. You'd think a man of his age would've learned to tie a tie by now. Or at least, switch to bow ties."

Sensing that Mary's train of thought was about to derail, I suggested (tactfully, mind you) that perhaps we could discuss Herbie's peculiarities some other time, like maybe the twelfth of never. An obliging Mary agreed.

"Anyway, as I started to tell you, it was the day of the big sale, and we were flooded with customers thanks to Denny's brilliant ad campaign. It was his best one yet if I say so myself. Wouldn't you agree?"

"I certainly would," I lied. I wasn't about to admit that I could recall neither the campaign nor the sale, but I knew if I let her talk Mary would eventually fill in the blanks.

"When Denny first brought up the idea of having a retro sale, I thought he was crazy. I never imagined that so many people who went to Seville High during the 1960s would show up. And with their class rings, no less. Personally, I think getting an additional fifty percent off on certain sale items had a lot to do with it."

So far, I hadn't learned anything from Mary other than England's Fine Furniture had another successful sale, thanks to her husband Denny's unflagging ingenuity. The male half of this Jack Spratt couple could sell pocket combs to nudists.

"I'm glad everything went so well and you had a good turnout. Were there any surprises?" I asked.

Mary's big, blueberry-colored eyes opened wide. "Surprises? Like what?"

"Oh, you know," I countered, "like did Kurt Summerfield turn up with Dona Deville on his arm?" It was a facetious question and I really didn't expect an answer.

I spent my high school years as a student at Little Flower Academy for Girls, a Catholic institution that was strong on education and weak on social activities. The way the good nuns saw it, if Adam had kept his distance, the incident between Eve and the serpent might have been avoided. The prospect of being a wallflower for the next four years was enough to make me tag after Mary and her public school crowd. Together, we attended almost every after-school activity sponsored by Seville High, where Mary and her twin brother, Charlie, were enrolled.

It was at one such function that Mary and I fell madly in love with the star of Seville High's varsity basketball team. The fact that the boy, Kurt Summerfield, was unaware of our existence failed to dampen our ardor. Our young hearts were crushed when, as king of the prom, Kurt selected Dona Deville to be his queen. We were convinced that he had been unduly influenced by the leggy cheerleader's movie-star looks and pinup girl figure.

The royal couple graduated a few weeks later. When the new school year began in the fall, Kurt was no longer part of our world. He had been replaced on the basketball court, and in our young hearts, by Norbert Finklestein. It was a true case of the king is dead; long live the king.

While Kurt dropped off the town gossips' radar after leaving Seville for parts unknown, the beautiful Dona popped up two decades later as the owner of Dona's Den, an exclusive Indianapolis health spa catering to the rich and famous. To my knowledge, no one from Seville had crossed the threshold of the tony establishment, or Dona's path, which is why I was stunned by Mary's reply to my question.

"Kurt didn't show up, but Dona did. She's still gorgeous and her shape is like, wow! Bet you'll never guess who she asked about," said Mary, holding her ice-tea glass aloft. "I'll give you a hint. It wasn't Kurt Summerfield."

"How the heck would I know. Probably Herbie Waddlemeyer. If nothing else, the guy is unforgettable."

"No, silly. Herbie was homeschooled. Besides, she didn't have to ask about him. She was standing right next to him when he got his tie caught. Honestly, Gin, sometimes I don't think you listen very well. I said you'd never guess. She asked about Charlie."

"Charlie? My Charlie? Why in the world would she ask about him? Unbelievable." Charlie was a late bloomer. By the time he'd morphed into the handsome guy who won my heart, Dona was long gone from Seville. "Unbelievable," I said again.

"Hey, I thought so, too," said Mary, "until

Dona explained everything. She said she'd heard all kinds of nice things about the redesign of the Sleepy Hollow Country Club main dining room before seeing it for herself. She couldn't recall the firm's name but remembered it had some connection to Charlie. That's why she asked about him. Luckily, Denny keeps a supply of your business cards on the counter, so he gave her one. I expected she'd call you and waited for you to say something but you didn't, so I didn't, either. Then, lo and behold, she called me this morning. She'd misplaced your card but had one of Denny's. Seeing that we're family, she asked if I would pass along her message." Mary stopped just long enough to take a needed breath and sip of ice tea. "Of course, I said yes. You know what I'm saying?"

"No, I don't." It was becoming difficult to hide my growing impatience. I'd had my fill of coffee and Mary certainly didn't need a third éclair. "You kind of lost me after you said something about explaining everything."

"Gosh, I'm sorry," Mary gushed, "it's just that I'm so excited for you. Imagine, Designer Jeans landing a contract with Dona Deville. See, I wasn't kidding when I said that it's your lucky day."

29

"Mary." I all but threw myself across the table. "Are you telling me that Dona Deville has been trying to get in touch with me, I mean Designer Jeans? When? How? Where? Am I supposed to call her or what? This is really, really unbelievable. And here I thought she was after Charlie!"

"My stars. Some sleuth you are," said Mary, alluding to my modest success in the realm of crime solving. "Sometimes the simplest thing confuses you. Now listen carefully, Gin. All you have to remember is that Dona Deville is going to phone you early next week. Monday or Tuesday. She needs an interior designer, and you need the work. Say, do you feel okay? You look kind of funny."

Leaning out of the booth, Mary flagged down the passing Tammie. "Be a lamb and get Mrs. Hastings an Irish coffee. Skip the cream, hold the sugar, and easy on the coffee."

"Got it, Mrs. E.," said the waitress, who had a penchant for reducing speech to the simplest of terms. "Celebratin' or medicinal, Mrs. H.?"

"A little of both," I groaned, rubbing my forehead with an ice cube taken from my untouched glass of water, "a little of both."

CHAPTER THREE

After leaving the club, I stopped at JR's and shared the "lucky day news" with my daughter and partner. Like her mother, JR was excited about the possibility of adding the Deville name to Designer Jeans' list of clientele. Returning home, I then began the excruciating long wait for the all-important phone call that, according to Mary, I would receive on either Monday or Tuesday.

A pessimist at heart, when I hadn't heard from Ms. Deville by Tuesday noon, I was convinced that Mary had unknowingly mixed up the message and Designer Jeans had missed out on what could have been a prestigious and lucrative contract. I was about to fix lunch when, to my surprise, the phone rang and I found myself speaking directly to the health spa proprietress.

Not one to waste time, Dona Deville was all business and only marginally polite. She quickly informed me that she'd recently inherited some property from her late aunt. Located on the northern edge of Seville, the property was close to the interstate and the old railroad station. The inheritance consisted of a few acres of scrubland along with three structures: a vintage cottage, a weather-beaten barn, and a large shed. The cottage faced Old Railway Road and was separated from the barn and shed by a thick clump of trees. The two outbuildings could be accessed via a rutted dirt-and-gravel side road.

"What do you have in mind for the property? A quick fix and cleanup job? If that's the case, I can put you in touch with a local man who handles that sort of thing." Despite what I'd said to Mary about competing with old man Wilson, I had no intention of doing so.

"Not really," said Dona. "The barn and shed are out of the picture, so to speak. They've been leased to a Mr. Abner Wilson. Perhaps you've heard of him. He pays the rent on time, keeps to himself, and asks for nothing. The perfect tenant, wouldn't you agree?"

Before I had a chance to respond, Dona stated her desire to turn the cottage into a personal weekend retreat. "After seeing what you've done with Sleepy Hollow's main dining room, I must say I was impressed. Returning the room to its original Art Deco decor was very clever of you."

I attempted to thank her for the compliment only to be rudely interrupted by Dona's announcement that I was being put on hold while she took another call. To pass the time I emptied the dishwasher, made a fresh pot of coffee, and sorted a mountain of junk mail. It was when I started to alphabetize my grocery list that I decided I'd lingered long enough in telephone limbo. I was about to return the bright pink monstrosity to its base when Dona Deville came back on the line.

"Gawd," wailed the insensible woman, "with all his money, the man could build his own spa. Instead, he keeps trying to buy mine. I told him to get a haircut. He was still laughing when I hung up on him, but that's the Donald for you."

Although I lacked confirmation, I was reasonably sure that the bothersome caller wasn't Donald Pumfreys, Seville's animal control officer.

"Well now, where were we?" snapped Dona. "Oh yes, I was about to ask if you're interested in taking on the project. Yes or no? Hello? Are you there, Mrs. Hastings?"

"Yes, I'm here," I stammered. Exhaling

sharply, I put Dona Deville's famous caller out of my mind and regained my composure. "I can't give you an answer without seeing the place, and I generally don't do an initial walk-through unless accompanied by the prospective client. Can that be arranged?"

"If you insist, I suppose so," Dona replied in a tone cold enough to freeze the fur off a polar bear's backside. "I'll have to switch the call to my personal assistant, Marsha Gooding. Perhaps she can fit you into my busy schedule. Hold on." With that said, Dona, the prima donna, took her leave.

Waiting for the call to be transferred, I overheard someone say the words, "freakin' fool." Although I wasn't positive who had uttered them, I had a pretty good idea that her initials were D. D.

"You've reached extension one-three. I'm busy at the moment. Please leave your name and number and someone will return your call." The recorded message was followed by an irritating beep. After silently cursing all the busy people in the world, and being just a little jealous because I wasn't one of them, I gave my name and was about to leave Designer Jeans' number when a female voice came on the line.

"Hi, Goody here. Sorry 'bout that. I just

hate talking to a machine, don't you? They're so impersonal and never give you enough time to say what you really want to say. Know what I mean? Hang on a sec while I grab a mug of herbal tea, then we can talk."

Marsha Gooding, or Goody as she insisted I call her, was anything but cold or business-like. In fact, the personal assistant seemed deliberately intent on moving the conversation from a professional level to one that was warm, encompassing, and personal.

Without any encouragement from me, I soon learned from Goody that her boss's former marriage to Rufus Halsted, a less-than-successful real estate developer, was considered by Dona to be the second-biggest mistake of her life, the first being that she'd neglected to have Rufus (or Ruffy, as he prefers to be called) sign a prenuptial agreement. The tumultuous Halsted union managed to limp along until two years ago. That's when Todd Masters, a muscleman twenty years Dona's junior, signed on as her personal trainer, and Ruffy was served with divorce papers. According to the gossipy Goody, the dissolution of the marriage was neither friendly nor cheap.

"To make matters even worse, the gal who handles all Dona's PR stuff, Maxine Roberts, has been spotted after hours in the company of a certain muscle-bound meathead," sniped Goody before piously adding, "I hope and pray that the two aren't more than just friends. Unlike us 'Plain Janes,' Dona's never experienced rejection. At this point in her life, I'm not all that sure she could survive it. Perhaps getting the cottage decorated will keep her mind off her troubles, at least for a little while."

"If I'm not being too nosy," I found myself asking the loose-lipped Goody, "did the aunt die of old age?"

"Lord, no. Not that she wasn't as old as dirt. No, she got on the interstate going the wrong way and ended up colliding with a semi hauling a wide load. The truck driver survived but Dona's aunt was killed instantly. Word has it that she was decapitated."

"Dear God! What in the world caused her to make such a tragic and deadly driving error?" I wondered aloud.

"That's what Dona would like to know," replied Goody. "The aunt was on her way back to Indy after visiting the cottage. In spite of her advanced age, the old gal was mentally and physically fit. Dona still frets about the accident even though everyone, including yours truly, has told her to forget it. It's time to move on."

Maybe Dona didn't heed the advice, but I did. Switching hats, I was all business, steering Goody back to the business of selecting a date, time, and place for my meeting with her boss.

"Hey, it looks like you're in luck, Jean. Maxine has Dona scheduled for a book-signing gig next Saturday at the grand opening of the new Lowell's Book Nook in Seville. I'll pencil you in to meet us there around three. She should be done by then. Now, what were we talking about? Oh yes, Dona of course," said Goody before adding with a snicker, "wait 'til you get a load of Ellie, the daughter. Talk about the apple falling far from the tree. She's not even in the orchard."

I could tell from the gleefulness in her voice, Goody was about to out another Deville skeleton from the closet. Since the time, date, and place of my meeting with Dona had been settled, I interrupted Marsha Gooding's latest soliloquy with the old chestnut of someone knocking at my door. As fibs go, it wasn't the most imaginative but it did bring the phone call to a merciful end.

Lighting a cigarette, I mentally reviewed my conversations with both women. I don't know what bothered me more — Dona Deville's aloofness or Marsha Gooding's unbidden candor.

Replacing dark thoughts with sunny ones, I pulled out my workbooks and began making speculative plans to turn the cottage into a weekend getaway that even a certain Donald would envy.

CHAPTER FOUR

Immersed in a variety of cottage design, I did my best to ignore Pesty's demand for lunch, but when she dropped her food dish on my foot, I gave up. "Okay, you win," I said, "but I hope you realize that you're not getting mac 'n' cheese, pizza, or any of your people-food favorites. I'm afraid it's Dandy Diet dog food for you, my fussy friend. And forget about dessert. It's been deleted from your menu."

"You better have something better than that planned for me, otherwise I'll be forced to go to Max's Diner for a bowl of his chili. From what I hear, it's even better than the clam chowder," Charlie said as he made his way into the kitchen from the attached garage, "and not quite as deadly."

That the dumpy diner was once again up and running came as a surprise to me. The previous fall, Max's clam chowder played a pivotal role in my effort to bring a blackmailing murderer to justice. Thanks to good timing by Matt Cusak (JR's police lieutenant husband), along with Doc Parker's medical skills, I survived being held captive by the killer and an almost fatal case of food poisoning.

"If you want to put your life on the line and eat at Max's, that's your choice, chum. Personally, if I were you, Charlie, I'd go with the dog food. But, if you'll give me a minute," I said, pushing my workbooks and notes aside, "I'll fix us some chicken salad sandwiches, fresh fruit, and ice-cold lemonade. Play your cards right, fella, and I might even throw in dessert. How does warm apple pie with a slice of cheese sound to you?"

Wrapping his muscular arms around me, Charlie pulled me close, so close that I could smell the faint aroma of shower gel on his deeply tanned skin and the hint of shampoo in his closely cropped, silvery hair.

"And everyone thought I married you for your money," he teased, tickling my neck with a long line of short kisses.

Fearing that her lunch was about to be usurped, the little Kees voiced her objection in a series of growling barks. After promising Charlie a rain check for his romantic overture, I got down to the business of feeding the hungry, myself included.

Like his twin sister, Mary, Charlie has a passion for sweets. Helping himself to a pre-lunch dessert of vanilla and caramel swirl ice cream, he casually mentioned that we were to be at our daughter's house no later than six p.m.

"Oh no," I yelped, accidentally dropping a large glob of mayonnaise into the waiting mouth of an certain opportunistic Keeshond. "It completely slipped my mind." The "it" was the bon-voyage backyard barbecue that JR and Matt were hosting for Dr. and Mrs. Parker. The Parkers were leaving the following day for Los Angeles, the first leg of an extended Hawaiian vacation. In his absence, Doc's patients would be cared for by young Dr. Peter Parker, his bachelor nephew who'd recently relocated from Indianapolis to Seville.

"I suppose," said Charlie as he transferred a spoonful of ice cream from his dish to the drooling Pesty's food bowl, "that the two deli trays you promised to make for the party at JR's this evening also slipped your mind."

"Jeez, you got that right. Actually, this whole Dona Deville business has thrown me a bit off-kilter," I said, hiding my misgivings regarding the prospective project

41

behind what I hoped was a sunny smile.

"I figured as much after overhearing your side of the phone conversation," said Charlie, "so when I saw you hauling out your workbooks, I ducked out to Milano's and picked up two party-size antipasto trays."

Milano's is a family owned and operated Seville restaurant that features authentic Italian cuisine. Even on my best day, I could never whip up a tray as good as one from Milano's.

"When I dropped them off at JR's," Charlie continued, "she said to tell you thanks. She also said not to mention anything about the Deville project in front of Matt. According to JR, after tonight's shindig, Matt wants her to slow down and take it easy for a while."

JR's husband, Matthew Cusak, grew up in a series of foster homes. At seventeen, he joined the United States Marine Corps. When his four-year stint was over, Matt bounced around the country, and from job to job, before enrolling at Indiana University where he met and fell in love with JR.

Shortly after graduation day, Matt and JR were married. While Matt pursued a career in law enforcement with the Seville police department, JR settled into the role of full-time wife and mother. The addition of

Designer Jeans to JR's hectic schedule is something that Matt has struggled with since day one. That he wanted JR to cut back on her workload wasn't exactly a surprise to me or something new.

"My lips are sealed," I assured Charlie as I set the table for the promised lunch. "By the way, you really are a prince. Taking care of the two trays qualifies you for a reward. Can you think of anything that you would really, really like?"

The question was barely out of my mouth when I knew the answer. Handing my husband a napkin, I instructed him to wipe the grin, and the ice cream, off his royal face.

CHAPTER FIVE

Instead of sealing my lips, I should have sealed my brain since the party and the trays weren't the only things that had slipped my mind. Because of my failure to remember that the washing machine was in dire need of a service call, I was left with a laundry chute filled with soiled clothes (mostly mine) and one very clean, very green chenille jumpsuit. Having no other choice, and looking like a hormonal Peter Pan, I zipped up the jumpsuit, strapped on a pair of sandals, drenched myself from head to toe with insect repellent and announced to the impatiently waiting Charlie that, at long last, I was good to go.

The drive from Kettle Cottage on Blueberry Lane to Matt and JR's 1920s renovated bungalow on Tall Timber Road took less time than it did for me to get dressed. Unfortunately, every parking space was filled. It took a bit of doing but Charlie eventually found a parking spot that was within walking distance of the party. That it was also within walking distance of the Himalayas was something I thought best not to mention. Besides, I had enough to do trying to remain upright while dislodging an accumulation of pebbles from my sandal-clad tootsies as we trudged along the dusty, unpaved road. By the time we reached our destination, I'd developed a couple of nasty blisters along with a new appreciation of Hannibal's trek over the Alps.

Kerry and Kelly, JR and Matt's nine-year-old twins, had been given the task of presenting each guest with a colorful, fragrant lei. The two kids spotted us the moment we entered the backyard.

"Hi, Grandma. Hi, Grandpa," said the flaxen-haired Kerry almost shyly and in stark contrast to her twin brother's boisterous shouts of "Aloha, Grandma and Grandpa. That's hula talk for hello and come back again," crowed the grinning Kelly before being corrected by his almost-always-correct twin sister.

"Aloha is a Hawaiian word." Kerry snorted, rolling her pale blue eyes in a show of exasperation. "Sometimes brothers are so dumb. There's no such thing as hula talk. Tell him, Grandma," ordered the pint-size feminist.

"Well," I said, accepting a wreath of red and white flowers from Kelly, whose mood was in danger of becoming as dark as his hair, "Hawaii is a collection of Polynesian islands, which explains the great diversity found in Hawaiian culture. That being the case, hula talk could very well be a collection of colloquialisms used by those who, over an extended period of time, have developed their own particular version of their native tongue. Any questions?"

"Nah," a smirking Kelly replied.

Just as I'd hoped, the gobbledygook explanation had defused a potentially explosive situation.

Satisfied that he'd been exonerated, the boy was ready to move on. "See ya later, alligators."

"Yeah, after a while, crocodiles," added Kerry with a conspiratorial wink to her twin, signaling a temporary truce in their ongoing, gender-driven battle of sibling rivalry.

Once Kerry and Kelly were out of hearing range, Charlie gave me a thumbs-up. "Nicely done, sweetheart. You sounded just like Judge Judy. By the way, you look rather striking this evening. Is that a new outfit? It sure is green."

"You should have quit while you were ahead, chum. Come on, Captain Hook, let's join the party before it's time for me to return to Neverland."

"Huh?" said a puzzled Charlie, leaving me to conclude that sometimes husbands, like brothers, are so dumb.

The crowd had spread across the redbrick patio and onto the lawn like warm syrup on a stack of hotcakes. Under a canopy of shade trees, an ice-filled copper washtub held an assortment of canned soda, fruit drinks, bottled water, and beer. Off to the far right, on an apron of flagstone, sat an oversized stainless-steel gas grill.

Picnic tables with bright, floral-patterned cloths had been strategically placed in close proximity to the white, ivy-covered gazebo. The low stone wall encircling the property looked party perfect with its thick blanket of climbing roses, clematis, and honeysuckle vines.

Although it was still early in the evening, the air was heavy with the delicious mixture of simmering barbecue sauce, molasses-soaked beans, blooming flowers, and the lemony scent of burning citric candles.

Once we'd exchanged pleasantries with half the neighborhood and had been formally introduced to Dr. Peter Parker, a pleasant but rather nondescript young man, Charlie made a beeline for his golf buddies and a cold beer. Without my husband's arm to lean on, I hobbled over to the gazebo where Doc Parker's wife, Lucy, was holding court.

"Ever since his fiancée died, quite needlessly I might add, the poor boy has thrown himself into his work," Lucy was saying as I sat down between JR and Mary on one of the several benches that line the inside walls of the little summerhouse. Thankfully, good manners prevailed and no one commented on my jumpsuit or limping gait.

JR was wearing a beige silk shirt and white jeans. A taupe-colored ribbon held her blond ponytail in place. She look both comfortable and chic. Mary had on a denim A-line skirt paired with a white and navy cotton wraparound blouse. Like JR, Mary looked great, proving that you don't have to be built like a swizzle stick to be fashionably dressed.

"Needlessly?" boomed the Amazonian Patti Crump in spite of sitting within whispering distance of Lucy. "What does that mean? Did she kill herself?" Like Sergeant Friday of television fame, Seville's first, and so far, only, female police officer was interested in the facts and just the facts, ma'am. If the older woman was intimidated by Patti's directness, it didn't stop her from continuing with the story.

Dressed in a beige linen shift that was almost as wrinkled as her skin, Lucy Parker heaved a deep sigh. "In a way, I guess you could say that, with her being anorexic and all. The girl certainly needed a lot more help than anyone, including Peter, suspected."

"And where and when did this all happen?" demanded the imposing Patti, ignoring the shushing sounds emitting from tiny Martha Stevens, the sharp-witted, Cuban-born wife of Rollie Stevens, Seville's antiquated police chief.

"Oh my, let me think a minute," begged Lucy, obviously pleased to be the center of attention. "She died three years ago. I believe it was on Valentine's Day. The poor girl was so emaciated that the family decided not to have the usual visitation and funeral. Schubert's in Indianapolis handled the cremation. Of course, Peter was just devastated."

"What an extraordinary way to die," exclaimed Mary. The concept of deliberately depriving oneself of food was almost beyond her comprehension. "I suppose that Peter, being a doctor as well as her fiancé, probably blamed himself for not being able to help the girl."

"Certainly not," replied Lucy sounding as offended as she looked. "If you want to know the truth, Peter blamed the girl's obsession with her weight on that silly book *Be Thin and Win,* by that awful woman, Dona Deville. Peter was so angry that he . . ." The rest of Lucy's reply was drowned out by the clanging of the dinner bell.

"Come and get it," yelled Matt between clangs. With a mountain of mouthwatering ribs, crocks of homemade baked beans, Papa Milano's antipasto trays, and a dessert table to die for, the subject of death by eating disorder was all but forgotten, at least for the time being.

JR, Mary, and Patti rushed off to help Matt with the dispensing of food while I limped across the lawn and into the house in search of a couple of Band-Aids for my blistered heels. As expected, I found what I needed in the downstairs green-and-white subway-tiled bathroom.

In most homes the bathroom is nothing special, but that's not the case with JR's bathroom. Everything about the room reflects the unpretentious look promoted by the Arts and Crafts movement, which began in England during the latter part of the nineteenth century. It's a style perfectly suited for JR's relaxed personality.

It took a while, but eventually Matt and JR had restored the room to its original, no-nonsense look. Like they say, everything old is new again, which would include the claw-foot bathtub and freestanding washbasin. The Craftsman-style makeover brought the bathroom into the twenty-first century while retaining the flavor of its Arts and Crafts origins.

On a glass shelf above the commode sits JR's small collection of Overbeck painted porcelain. Dubbed by Mary Overbeck, one of six sisters who owned and operated Over-beck Pottery from 1911 to 1955 in Cam-bridge City, Indiana, as "humor of the kiln," the little figurines add a touch of whimsy to the room's otherwise uncluttered design and decor.

Reaching inside the square wall-mounted, bevel-mirrored medicine cabinet, I inadver-tently knocked over a plastic container from Finklestein's Pharmacy. Even without the aid of my misplaced cheaters, I recognized JR's name on the prenatal vitamin prescrip-tion. The accidental discovery of the pre-scription renewed my determination to stay on the sunny side of the street. In the meantime, JR's secret was safe with me.

By Saturday morning, my resolve to remain positive had considerably waned. From past experience, I knew the importance of establishing a good rapport with a prospective client. It was something that my phone conversation with Dona Deville hadn't accomplished. Knowing the lady was less than thrilled with my insistence that she accompany me on the walk-through, I had a sinking feeling that I wasn't on Dona's list of favorite people.

With the added fear that the cottage might be on the brink of structural disaster, the sunny side of the street was growing darker by the minute. Something had to be done and done fast to quiet my nerves and steady my shaky positive attitude.

Charlie had already left for his golf match with Denny and most likely wouldn't be home until the late afternoon. Since I was in complete agreement with Matt's wish for JR to do less, I reached for the phone and called Mary.

"Hey, Mar, it's Jean. How would you like it if I treated you to the all-you-can-eat breakfast buffet at Farmer John's?"

"My stars, I'd love it, but knowing you," Mary said with a giggle, "I'd say that you have an ulterior motive. Does it have anything to do with sleuthing? I hope not, otherwise our husbands will have our heads on platters, and I don't even want to think about what Matt will do to us."

Even though she would have denied it, I could tell that Mary was disappointed upon learning my ulterior motive involved nothing more dangerous or exciting than a short side trip to Dona's cottage on Old Railway Road. With both the cottage and the restaurant located near the same interstate, the drive from one place to the other would be a relatively short one.

"But why this morning?" asked Mary. "I thought you and Dona had a date to go to the cottage after the book signing today at Lowell's. What did she do? Change her mind?"

Before I could answer, Mary prattled on. "Did you read Hilly Murrow's review of Dona's new book in this morning's edition of the *Seville Sentinel*? If Peter Parker was upset over *Be Thin and Win,* he'll probably go ballistic over *Dump Your Doctor.* According to Hilly, the new book is chock-full of home remedies that can cure just about everything from athlete's foot to zits. She gave it four stars so I guess she really likes it."

"Yeah, whatever," I said, anxious to move the conversation away from local reporter

Hilly Murrow's critique of Dona's latest book and back to the reason for my phone call. "Mary, even though we probably won't be able to get inside the cottage, I need to at least take a look at the outside before meeting with Dona. It may very well be in such a state of disrepair that I won't even want the job."

"My stars, I've never known you to be so nervous about doing an initial walk-through. What's your problem?"

I wasn't about to admit to Mary that my inherited Irish intuition was acting up again. Along with fraying my nerves, it had also cost me a good night's sleep.

"Hey, no problem," I said with forced gaiety, "it's just that I don't want to be surprised if it turns out the place needs a structural engineering firm more than it needs Designer Jeans. What we find out there might end up killing the whole deal."

At the time, I hadn't the slightest inkling that my words would turn out to be so prophetic.

CHAPTER SIX

A cool front had crept down from the north the previous night, bringing with it a small measure of relief from the normally hot, humid summer weather. With an expected high temperature of only seventy-five degrees, a northern breeze, and partially cloudy skies, it was a suitable day to invite Pesty along for the ride.

Spurred on by the prospect of being with Mary, who is known to keep a supply of cookies in her purse, and with hopes of being the recipient of a Farmer John's doggy bag, the short-legged Kees made the leap from driveway to van in a single bound. Exhausted by the Superman-like feat, Pesty settled down for a morning nap.

Ever the optimist, Mary put Herbie Waddlemeyer in charge of England's Fine Furniture and was waiting for me at the store's delivery entrance. In spite of making a few wrong turns (unlike Charlie, I don't have a compass in my nose or in my vehicle) Mary and I were soon truckin' on down Old Railway Road.

While I concentrated on avoiding an endless series of potholes, Mary drank in the scenery, which consisted of not much more than some tumbledown fences, fallow fields, groves of leafy trees, and large patches of prairie grass.

"You know something, Gin," Mary remarked as I maneuvered the van around a particularly nasty pothole, "I can't remember the last time I was on this road. Can you?"

"Yeah, but it was years ago when JR attended summer camp. They had a field trip out to the old railroad station and JR signed up for it. Had I known Herbie Waddlemeyer would be driving the bus, I never would have volunteered to go along."

"Why on earth not? The man's an excellent driver," said Mary, coming to her employee's defense. "He's never had an accident or even a ticket. Honestly, Gin, sometimes you're so judgmental."

"Well, you would be, too, if you had to spend two hours on a hot bus with no one to talk to except Herbie," I said, steering the van around the rotting remains of unrecognizable roadkill. "I missed the entire tour thanks to him and his big, fat head."

"What in the world does the size of Herbie's head have to do with your missing the tour and spending two hours on the bus?" asked the bewildered Mary.

"Because, my dear Watson, that's how long it took me to free Herbie's oversized noggin from the clutches of the automatic door. At the time, I thought it was a freak accident," I added before changing the subject. "Keep an eye out for some sign of civilization like a mailbox or a driveway. Somebody, either Dona Deville, or maybe it was her personal assistant, said the place faces Old Railway Road. Supposedly, it's not far from the old railroad station and the interstate."

"I don't see anything like that, but I just saw a sign for getting on the interstate so we must be pretty close," said Mary before shouting, "Oh my stars, there it is! There's the cottage!"

Thanking God for Mary's keen eyesight and the van's new set of brakes, I safely negotiated a quick turn onto the narrow gravel driveway that circled the property. After bringing the van to a halt in front of the cottage, I stepped out and looked around. There was something about the place that seemed vaguely familiar. I was baffled until I spotted the school bell and pole that stood just off to the right of the porch.

Surrounded on three sides by a thicket of mature trees and hidden somewhere beneath the peeling and faded red exterior with its mustard-colored trim was the building's original footprint. Once a humble center of learning, the little schoolhouse had since been transformed into a two-storied cottage. The architectural style was classic Stick.

The Stick style evolved from Carpenter Gothic, an offshoot of Victorian architecture popular in the mid- to late-nineteenth century. Purely American, Stick style is distinctive for its use of board-and-batten vertical siding minus the fussiness of classic and romantic ornamentation generally found in Victorian and Carpenter architecture.

The faded, reddish-brown front door had an overhead transom window of clear glass. Around the door someone had painted a border of hearts and flowers in the same mustard color that trimmed the windows, front porch, railings, and banisters. The porch ran the width of the cottage and like the cottage, it had a shake roof. A porch swing of faded red was to the left of the front door at a right angle to the door and a trio of faded, mustard-yellow-trimmed windows. The cottage sat on a foundation of fieldstone.

One look at the cottage's exterior and I immediately rid my mind of the blue, green, and gray palette along with the New England decor that I'd been considering. Instead, I visualized doing the cottage inside and out in an array of earth tones. I would paint the exterior in a medium shade of brown and in keeping with the earth-tone palette, all trim on the cottage would be done in a forest green. Wooden shutters of forest green would flank the windows and like the trim around the chocolate-colored front door, they would be decorated with hand-painted stenciled hearts and flowers in a pale yellow-green.

The existing porch swing, which sat at a right angle to the front door, would be given a fresh coat of forest green paint. A pair of green ladder-back rockers with thick cushions and a small wooden barrel with a checkerboard top would make the porch an inviting space to visit with friends or a place to kick back and relax.

The new palette would add warmth to a decor of welcoming simplicity and complement the woodland setting. It would also capture the spirit of individualism, a characteristic of American country charm.

I felt like a kid on Christmas Eve whose head is filled with wonderful visions of what was to come. Baskets of sunflowers, hand-hooked rugs, quilts, trestle tables, ladder-back chairs, hurricane lamps, framed samplers, green glassware, mason jars, stenciled borders, and open cabinetry danced in my head.

With a renewed sense of purpose and direction, I was delighted to discover that now I was actually looking forward to my meeting with Dona Deville.

Mary emerged from the van and walked over to where I was standing. "Hey, I think I know this place. This used to be the one-room schoolhouse that Great-Uncle Fortesque Hastings and his twin brother, Forsyth, attended as children. I've even got an old photo of the two of them ringing that bell. With the outside being so changed, I'm dying to see the inside, aren't you, Gin?"

"Sure, but I'll bet you an extra-large mocha latte from the Koffee Kabin that the place is locked up tighter than an all-night liquor store safe." The Koffee Kabin, Seville's answer to Starbucks, brews a wickedly delicious mocha latte.

"You're on," Mary said, flashing a

dimpled, mischievous smile. "Last one on the porch is a rotten egg."

Moving faster than either one of us thought possible, the race to the porch ended in a dead heat. When I stopped to catch my breath, Mary reached for the doorknob and gave it a twist. To my surprise, the door was unlocked.

"I do believe that a certain somebody owes me a mocha latte. Extra large, if I'm not mistaken," said Mary, crossing the threshold and stepping into the foyer.

Being a few steps behind, I was unable to prevent what happened next. First, Mary let loose with a bloodcurdling scream. Then she fainted. My faithful friend, the ingenuous Mary, had literally stumbled upon the dead body of a woman.

CHAPTER SEVEN

Faced with the prospect of moving Mary without disturbing the body, I looked around, hoping to find a nearby sofa or even an area rug on which to place Mary. But a quick glance at the foyer with its worn and faded painted checkerboard floor leading to the stair hall told me that the house was virtually empty. The only thing in the adjoining living room was a massive, field-stone fireplace. On the wide board pine floor was an old painted floor cloth that had seen better days.

Calling on muscles that I'd assumed had been permanently lost due to a combination of age and apathy, I managed to drag the unconscious Mary from the entrance hall and out to the front porch. I made an attempt to lift her limp form onto the porch swing only to discover that it was simply not possible. With the unresponsive Mary slipping from my grasp like a lump of Jell-O,

I decided it would be easier on both of us if I propped her up in a sitting position against the porch railing. Once that was done, I took off running for the van, where I grabbed Pesty's travel bowl of water. Gasping for breath, I sped back to Mary, doused her with the contents of the bowl, and prayed it would do the trick. It did.

"Oh my stars," cried Mary as her eyes fluttered open, "what happened? How come I'm all wet? Is it raining?"

"No, it's not raining, and you're wet because I threw water in your face, you know like they do in the movies when someone passes out. Joan Crawford did it all the time."

"I passed out? Now why in the world . . ." Mary stopped in midsentence, her peaches-and-cream complexion turning almost as white as her hair. "Oh no," she moaned, "it's all coming back to me. What a shock finding her like that."

"Her who?" It seemed unlikely that Mary could identify the dead woman, but I asked anyway. "You wouldn't happen to know her name by any chance, would you?"

"Of course I would, I mean I do," said the flustered and bedraggled Mary, "it's Dona Deville."

It was my turn to go into shock. Grabbing

a banister for support, I lowered my head, closed my eyes, and took a couple of deep breaths. I forced myself to pull myself together, at least for the time being. Only later, and in the privacy of Kettle Cottage, would I allow myself the luxury of falling apart.

"Maybe you should go back in there," suggested Mary, rolling her deep blue eyes in the direction of the foyer, "and check on her. Maybe she's not actually dead."

Although I'd had only a fleeting glimpse of the corpse, the ghastly image of the face with its gaping mouth, bulging eyes, and horribly bruised neck had burned itself into my brain.

"Let me put it to you this way, Mar. When was the last time someone greeted you at the door sprawled on the floor and looking like the Pale Rider on a very bad day? Trust me, the woman in there is definitely dead."

Gathering up what was left of my courage, and without so much as a backward glance at the body in the foyer, I closed the door of the cottage. Unlike Lot's wife, I wasn't tempted to take another look.

"Really, Gin," said Mary, following close behind me as I collected Pesty's bowl and made my way down the porch stairs, "was it necessary to use dog water to revive me? It seems to me that it would have been quicker and certainly a lot more sanitary to use water from the cottage."

"Jeez, Mary, I practically save your life, and what do I get for my effort? Unfounded criticism," I said, shaking my head. "Even an amateur sleuth like me knows better than to disturb a crime scene. As it is, our fingerprints are probably all over the front door, the entrance hall, the porch, and that jiggly porch swing." I should have come clean with Mary, confessing that what I'd said about not distrubing the crime scene and the presence of our fingerprints was purely an afterthought on my part. But I didn't. As afterthoughts go, I felt it was one of my best.

Returning to the van, a contrite Mary broke out her emergency supply of sugar cookies. While the two amigos (Mary and Pesty) munched their way to carb heaven, I used my cell phone and called the police. After promising the dispatcher that we would stay put until help arrived, I silently apologized to my ancestors for having doubted the power of Irish intuition and lit a badly needed cigarette.

Only when the normally passive Pesty began to growl softly did it occur to me that whoever was responsible for Dona Deville's demise might be lurking about. It was a frightening thought and one that I chose not to share with Mary. I figured that she'd had more than enough excitement for one day. Besides, Pesty's supply of water was running low.

What seemed like hours was in reality only a matter of minutes. With sirens screaming, two police cars (one marked and one unmarked) turned into the driveway, raising clouds of gray dust before coming to an abrupt halt behind the van.

I'd already imagined how things would probably unfold once my no-nonsense, police lieutenant son-in-law, Matt, and his trusty sidekick, Sergeant Sid Rosen, answered my call for help. Most likely, after checking that Mary and I were okay, the tall, dark, and handsome Matt would then instruct the mustaschioed, bald, and stoic Sid to take our statements before sending us merrily, or maybe not so merrily, on our way. With a bit of luck, Pesty might still be the happy recipient of a Farmer John's doggy bag. As far as I was concerned, the death of Dona Deville was a police matter and I had no intention of getting involved. Of course, everything changed when Police Chief Rollie Stevens, minus Matt and Sid, arrived on the scene.

With his red lips, raisin-like eyes, brown skin, woolly white hair, and chubby physique, the elderly Rollie looks more like the impish gingerbread man of nursery rhyme fame than Seville's top cop. But there was nothing impish about the man, or the gun he was holding, when he ordered me and Mary to get out of the van.

"Keep your hands where I can see 'em," instructed the chief as we scrambled to comply. "And I'll need to see some photo identification such as a valid passport."

"P . . . P . . . Passport?" Mary sputtered. "I have a driver's license but I don't have a passport. I almost got one last year when Denny told me we were going to visit a bunch of foreign countries, but when I found out they were all in Disney World's Epcot Center, I didn't bother. I never dreamed that I'd need a passport in my own hometown." Mary's eyes were about the size of dinner plates and her bottom lip had started to tremble, a sure sign of impending tears.

"Rollie Stevens, are you serious?" I'd almost said, "are you nuts?" but caught myself in time. "You know very well who we are and put that gun away before someone gets hurt."

Looking more than a bit sheepish, the old

policeman returned the weapon to its holster. "I've always wanted to nab a couple of female desperadoes before trading in my badge and gun for a set of wings and a harp. This was probably my last chance and now you've spoiled it."

The man looked and sounded so dispirited, I almost felt sorry for him. Most people his age had long ago retired. Thanks to the ironclad contract that the town council insisted he sign, the police chief had the final say as to if and when he would retire. In the meantime, he seemed content to let Matt run the show while he kept himself busy with raising awareness and funds for the many animal projects he supported. I couldn't even remember the last time that Rollie Stevens headed up a major investigation.

He repeated his request to see some identification, and I handed Rollie my driver's license. When he laughed out loud at my photo, any sympathy I might have harbored for the old gingerbread man crumbled. Maybe Rollie Stevens wasn't mad, but he certainly was maddening.

Finished with me and Mary for the moment, the chief turned his attention to the two patiently waiting uniformed officers. After quietly suggesting to Patti Crump that perhaps she could begin gathering evidence, Rollie Stevens ordered Jasper Merkle, a rookie on the force, to start photographing the crime scene.

"I want pictures of everything, especially close-up shots of the stiff. And Jasper, try not to move the body until after Sue Lin Loo has had a chance to check it over," Rollie said, pronouncing the medical examiner's full name as if it were one word. "She should be along within the hour, I hope."

Mary and I watched with Rollie Stevens as the slightly built, nervous Jasper Merkle hurried to catch up with the solidly built, confident Patti Crump. A string of expletives could be heard when the two officers entered the cottage. Judging from the high pitch of the voice, I guessed correctly that the obscenities had come from the rookie cop.

"I'd venture that about now," Rollie said with a chuckle, "young Jasper's sorry he gave up taking wedding pictures for this. Even the ugliest bride is better looking than a corpse. And smells a hellava lot better, too."

Still chuckling, the chief reached through the open passenger window of his unmarked police car and retrieved two containers of coffee along with a couple of napkin-wrapped doughnuts. Handing the coffee to me and the pastries to Mary, he then ordered us to return to the van and remain there until someone was available to take our statements.

"And just when the hell might that be?" I asked, knowing I sounded as irritated as I looked and felt.

"Your guess is as good as mine," Rollie called over his rounded, stooped shoulder as he headed for the cottage.

"Rollie Stevens, if you think a couple of stale doughnuts and some cruddy convenience-store coffee will be enough to turn me and Mrs. England into happy campers, then you're in for a big surprise."

Turning around, the chief quickly retraced his steps back to the van where Mary and I were seated. Sticking his round, brown face through the open driver's side window, a grinning Rollie Stevens politely informed me that I owed him three dollars for, as he put it, the java and sinkers.

While I contemplated the punishment for assaulting a police officer, Mary grabbed a crumpled bill from the van's console. Leaning across the seat, she passed the money to Rollie and magnanimously donated the change to the police chief's current favorite charity — Coats for Cats.

Rollie graciously thanked Mary for her generous contribution and headed back to the cottage with a smile on his lips, a spring in his step, and my twenty bucks in his pants pocket.

Resigned to the fact that we probably wouldn't be leaving anytime soon, I took a swig of the lukewarm coffee and lit a cigarette. Within seconds of doing so, I found myself listening to another pitch from Mary about the patch. As if on cue, and despite the open windows and the steady breeze that kept the van relatively smoke-free, Pesty began to sneeze. Stubbing out the half-smoked cigarette, I glared at the crumb-encrusted duo and wondered if they knew how close they'd come to sharing the same fate as a certain health spa owner.

Finishing the truly awful-tasting coffee, I flipped open my cell phone. Without the aid of the perpetually missing reading glasses, I eventually was able to speed dial JR's home phone.

Although modern technology identified me as the caller, JR relied on personal experience to identify the purpose of my call. Without so much as a "hello" she proceeded to do just that. Or so she thought.

"Okay, Mother, you're having trouble deciding what to wear to your little tête-à-

71

tête with Dona Deville. So what else is new? Since you obviously need my advice, I'll give it to you. Wear anything but that green jumpsuit. It makes you look like the Jolly Green Giant. Ho, ho, ho."

"Very funny, JR. For your information, your father happens to like that outfit." I waited until she stopped laughing before giving her a fast rundown on all that had taken place, beginning with Mary's gruesome discovery and ending with the police chief's answer as to when we would be free to leave.

To say that JR was surprised and shocked would be an understatement.

"Oh m'god, Mother. How awful. Is there anything I can do to help you and Aunt Mary?"

"Yes, do me a favor and get ahold of Matt. Tell him I don't want to solve the crime. I just want to go home. Mary's out of cookies, Pesty's out of water, and I'm out of sorts."

"Sorry, Mom, no can do. Matt and Sid Rosen are in the middle of an important investigation and that's about all I can say. I'm afraid that this time, you're on your own."

I was about to hang up when JR made me an offer that sounded pretty good under the circumstances.

"I know it's not exactly the kind of help you were looking for, but how about if I get in touch with Pops and Uncle Denny, explain the situation, and invite them to have dinner with me and the twins tonight. I'm making spaghetti. You and Aunt Mary are invited, too, of course. We'll eat around five thirty or six, depending on when everyone can get here."

"Thanks, JR, I really appreciate it," I said. "Your father took his cell phone when he left for his golf match with Uncle Denny so you should be able to reach him. If you run into a problem, give me a call on my cell phone."

"Will do. And, Mom, I'm sorry for making fun of the green jumpsuit. You always look good no matter what you wear. Gotta go. Love ya. Bye."

Despite Matt not being available to rescue me, the call to JR brightened my outlook. The thought of sharing dinner with family appealed to me a lot more than solving a grisly murder, which is what a certain, rather wacky police chief was going to have to do. In addition to my twenty dollars, Rollie Stevens also had my sympathy, and this time he could keep it.

CHAPTER EIGHT

Checking the clock on the van's dashboard, I was surprised to find that it was still relatively early in the day. Thinking back, I mentally reviewed the timeline of when we'd arrived at the cottage and discovered the body. I'd picked up Mary around nine o'clock and it had taken us about half an hour to find the cottage. Even though I didn't recall the exact time, I was pretty sure that I'd phoned the police sometime between nine thirty-five and nine forty. Since we didn't see any vehicles on Old Railway Road, and assuming the killer didn't bother to stick around, I was guessing that the murder occurred no later than nine twenty-five. The problem with the timeline was that it ended without a clue as to when or how Dona had gotten to the cottage. If she came via automobile, was it hers? If so, then where was the car? Did the killer take it?

Mary and Pesty had fallen asleep. Taking

advantage of the situation, I relit my cigarette and contemplated the glut of questions that were swirling around in my head like confetti in a wind tunnel.

I was deep in thought when Dr. Loo and two medical technicians arrived in Loo's oversized black SUV. The SUV filled the remaining section of the drive leading to the highway. The trio exited the vehicle and were headed for the cottage when Loo instructed the two young men to go ahead, stating that she would be along in a moment. She waited until the techs entered the cottage before strolling over to the van.

"Mrs. Hastings, don't you have better things to do with your time than finding dead bodies? I'm beginning to think Lieutenant Cusak's right when he says your middle name is trouble."

"Well, he's wrong. For your information, Sleeping Beauty over there," I said, pointing to Mary who was sawing wood, as was Pesty, "discovered the body all by herself. The only thing I did was to get Mary out of there as fast as I could and then I phoned the police."

The petite brunette with the almond-shaped eyes and engaging smile looked more like a beauty pageant winner than a highly capable and respected medical examiner. "And now you're hanging around for what? Hoping the murderer returns to the scene of the crime so you can capture him or her? Most of them don't, you know."

"Actually, we'd be long gone by now if Chief Stevens had someone available to take our statements," I replied. "And yes, I most certainly do have better things to do than being stuck at a crime scene," I added, deliberately ignoring her remarks regarding returning murderers and their capture.

"I'm sure that you do. All kidding aside, my mom almost lost it when my dad was laid up. Perhaps you'll do better, although I think all men are lousy patients. Good luck," said Loo, turning away from the van.

"Hey, wait a minute," I called out to the medical examiner as she sprinted up the porch stairs. "Good luck with what? I don't understand what you're talking about." But by then Dr. Sue Lin Loo had disappeared into the cottage.

Stymied by Loo's comments, I was struggling to make sense of the conversation when the cottage door opened and out walked Patti Crump, tape recorder in hand. At long last, Mary and I were finally going to give our statements and be on our way. It was too late for breakfast and a tad early for lunch but we had a good chance of making it to the brunch buffet at Farmer John's. I could almost smell the three-cheese omelet, sausages, sourdough toast, bread pudding, and fresh coffee. Apparently, I wasn't the only one.

"My stars," Mary remarked, rubbing the sleep from her eyes, "I had the most terrible dream. We were in the buffet line at Farmer John's and just when it was our turn to be served, they ran out of food. Rollie Stevens came out of the kitchen wearing nothing but a chef's hat and apron. He said the only thing left was some dog water and Dona's dead body. When we tried to leave, he threw stale doughnuts and cold coffee at us. It was just horrible."

"Yeah, it sounds like it, especially the part about Rollie and the chef's hat and apron."

Between Dr. Loo's comments and Mary's dream, I felt like Alice in Wonderland. The only thing missing was the red queen threatening to cut off our heads. Instead, Patti Crump, looking almost as grim as Carroll's maniacal monarch, ordered us out of the van and onto the porch.

"Come on, Mar," I said, "it's time for us to go through the looking glass. Should you see any cookies, don't eat 'em."

If nothing else, Patti Crump was efficient. In no time flat, Mary and I had given our statements and were informed by Patti that we were free to leave. Even though I was anxious to do just that, the three vehicles parked around us made it virtually impossible.

"Wait in your van," instructed Patti, a former heavy equipment operator, "while I jockey the other vehicles out of your way. They gotta be moved anyway, seein' that the chief called Morty Butterworth of Stanford Motors to get a tow truck out here on the double."

"Why on earth did he do that?" I commented aloud without adding that given the situation, a call for a hearse would have been more appropriate.

Since Patti, who'd reentered the cottage to collect the necessary sets of keys, either hadn't heard my question or had purposely ignored it, Mary took it upon herself to provide me with the obvious answer.

"My stars, Gin. What's happened to your logic? Why does anyone call for a tow truck? Because, you silly goose, they need something towed."

"Jeez, now why didn't I think of that? Thank you, Mary, thank you." Jumping out of the van, I all but ran to the backyard of the cottage where the late-model silver Cadillac with the DIET GAL vanity plate was parked. I now had the answer as to how Dona Deville had gotten to the cottage, but the when and the why still eluded me. I also knew that as a lifelong jigsaw puzzle junkie, I wouldn't rest until all the pieces were in place.

CHAPTER NINE

We arrived at Farmer John's shortly after eleven o'clock and were seated immediately. Unlike Mary's dream, there wasn't a dead body or a crazy cop in sight. Being almost as hungry as Mary, I made short work of what can only be described as a sumptuous three-course brunch. Once Mary had polished off a second generous helping of peach cobbler, and I had a napkin stuffed with enough tidbits to satisfy a certain four-legged eating machine, we were back in the van and headed for home.

While I was mulling over the events of the morning, Mary busied herself with the radio. Finding nothing to her liking on any of the FM stations, she switched to the AM ones.

"For chrissake, Mary, either pick something or shut the darn thing off." I'd barely gotten the words out of my mouth when I heard the grating voice of Seville's star reporter, Hilly Murrow, slicing through the stream of static. "Don't touch that dial," I yelled, pushing Mary's hand away from the radio.

"Well, excuse me," a miffed Mary replied, "I didn't realize that you're such a fan of local programming."

"I'm not but I would like to hear what's being said locally about Dona's death, seeing that we missed the news out of Indy while we were in Farmer John's. And I'm sorry that I yelled at you. Now, let's listen to Miss Know-It-All's take on things. If nothing else, she's opinionated."

Even though Hilly's report was light on facts and laced with innuendoes, I managed to glean from it that Dona's entire entourage, including Ellie and Rufus Halsted, Todd Masters, Maxine Roberts, and Marsha Gooding, had arrived in town Friday night. They, along with Dona, checked into an unspecified bed-and-breakfast establishment. Without disclosing where, when, or why, Hilly implied that she had been present when the Deville entourage learned of Dona's death. She used words such as devastated, stunned, grief-stricken, shocked, and heartbroken in describing the group's reaction to the news.

With an irritating voice that matched her

contentious personality, stick-thin body, and sharp facial features, the middle-age newshound droned on. According to Hilly, other than a certain young doctor who was a newcomer to Seville, everyone in town had been looking forward to seeing the health spa diva at the Book Nook.

The way Hilly carried on, one would think that the late Ms. Deville was a combination of Mother Teresa and Princess Diana. From my own brief telephone encounter with Dona, I felt a comparison to Marie Antoinette with a pinch of Cinderella's stepmother thrown in would have been more on target.

The young visiting doctor, again, according to Hilly, as well as the two local women who'd discovered the body were at the top of the police chief's short list of suspects.

I'd heard more than enough and was about to turn off the radio when Hilly mentioned a freak accident that had taken place on the thirteenth hole of the Sleepy Hollow golf course.

"Despite it being officially ruled as an accident," intoned the reporter in her best "I know something you don't know" voice, "I find it strange that the wives of the two men involved in the bizarre incident are the same two women who, for some unknown reason, were at the Deville crime scene and claim to have stumbled upon Dona's body. Chief Stevens had better watch his step with these rather slippery suspects. And that's my tip of the day. This is Hilly R. Murrow reminding you that what happens in Seville is always news to me."

"Talk about yellow journalism," Mary fumed, clicking off the radio. "I feel just like Jack Nicholson did in that movie when he demanded that Tom Cruise show him the truth."

I thought about straightening out Mary's mixed-up film dialog but since I agreed with the gist of what she'd said, I decided to let it go. Like Mary, I, too, was frustrated and upset with Hilly Murrow's version of the news. I also wanted to know more about what the reporter had referred to as a "bizarre incident" supposedly involving Charlie and Denny. Passing my cell phone to Mary, I asked her to give Charlie a call. When he failed to answer, she then called Denny.

From Mary's reaction to what her husband had to say, I surmised that some nincompoop had been accidentally struck by a golf ball. The unlucky guy was taken to the hospital via ambulance where Dr. Peter Parker confirmed that the ball had broken the man's kneecap. Only after Mary ended the call did I learn that the injured nincompoop and Charlie were one in the same.

Dr. Loo's remark about her parents and her belief that men were lousy patients finally made sense. Most likely, she'd been present when Charlie was admitted into the hospital and made the assumption that I'd been notified. No wonder she questioned my presence at the cottage.

Even though the traffic was light, the drive to Garrison General Hospital in Seville seemed to take forever. Everything, including my mood, had deteriorated. How much more could go wrong, I wondered as I pulled the van into the hospital's parking lot. I was about to find out. Stepping from the vehicle, Mary and I were drenched to the skin by a sudden, heavy downpour that seemed to come out of nowhere.

"You know something, Mary," I remarked as we splish-splashed our way across the lot's wet surface, "I don't think we're in Kansas anymore."

Three hours and about a half dozen cups of coffee later, Dr. Peter Parker came into the fourth-floor lounge with the news that Charlie's knee surgery was over and the prognosis for a complete recovery was quite good.

"Of course, he's going to require a great deal of care both before and after the cast is removed, especially since he's got his heart set on returning to the golf links ASAP," said Dr. Parker who, in spite of the hospital scrubs he was wearing, looked far too young to be a physician and surgeon. He also looked very, very tired. Despite not being the handsomest of men, Peter Parker, with his sandy-colored hair, sad brown eyes, and lopsided smile, had a certain average, all-American, apple-pie appeal.

"Mr. England," he said, focusing his attention on Denny, "is it true that Mr. Hastings's accident was the result of your tee shot going askew when a bee stung you on the buttocks?"

The affable, lanky Scotsman's ruddy complexion turned a deeper shade of red while his nearly bald head turned a pretty shade of pink. "Yeah," Denny replied, rubbing his crinkly blue eyes out of embarrassment rather than fatigue. "And you know what Charlie said just before he passed out from the pain? He said it served me right getting stung where I did 'cause I took so damn long setting up my tee shot. Now that's what I call a real golfer."

Apparently, the doctor was also a "real golfer" since he seemed to appreciate Denny's comment a whole lot more than either me or Mary. Personally, I felt that Ronald Reagan's remark about forgetting to duck would have covered things nicely.

After a final round of assurances from the doctor regarding Charlie's condition, followed by a round of my heartfelt thank-yous, Dr. Peter Parker took my hand in his and gave it a surprisingly strong squeeze. For a fleeting moment, I wondered if I'd just touched hands with a healer who was also a killer. I quickly dismissed the idea as being absurd. Just because his grip was powerful enough to crack walnuts, I told myself, it didn't mean that he was responsible for choking the life out of Dona Deville, which, judging from the black-and-blue marks I'd seen around her throat, was how she'd met her untimely end.

Throughout the remainder of the day and into the evening, Charlie drifted dreamily in and out of consciousness. Seeking to fill the void left by the departure of Mary and Denny (I insisted they keep the dinner date with JR), I turned on the wall-mounted television set. Engaged in channel surfing, I was unaware that someone had entered the room until I felt a hand on my shoulder. Thinking that it was JR, who planned on visiting her father later that evening, I

86

turned around in the small bedside chair and was suprised to find myself staring into the piercing dark eyes of Martha Stevens, the police chief's loyal and devoted wife.

Martha had more on her mind than visiting the sick. With her creamy complexion, trim body, and smartly styled gray hair, the diminutive woman, who'd fled her island home when Fidel Castro proved not to be the democratic savior of the people, looked and acted far younger than her sixty-five years.

While Charlie managed from time to time to let out a moan or flutter his eyelids, he continued to be pretty much out of it, which was a good thing since Martha was about to make me an offer that any wife with an ailing husband wouldn't refuse.

From personal experience, I knew all too well the truth of Dr. Loo's pronouncement that men were lousy patients. Last year when Charlie came down with a bad head cold and took to his bed for three days, I gave him round-the-clock care. In return, he gave me a hard time. I came close to serving him divorce papers along with the homemade chicken soup. By the time Doc Parker pronounced Charlie fit to return to the land of the living, I was half dead from exhaustion and had new respect for Florence Nightingale.

Martha, a semiretired registered nurse and licensed physical therapist, had come up with an ingenious plan that would protect her husband's reputation as Seville's top cop and pave the way for him to leave the force on a high note. The plan was as follows: In return for her providing my husband with in-home care and outpatient therapy, something crucial to Charlie's full and speedy recovery, I would provide her husband, Rollie, with a successful murder investigation, something crucial to his well-deserved, long-overdue retirement.

"Maybe some people, like my husband, don't want to admit it, but when it comes to figuring out a complicated murder, you are a regular Sherlock Holmes," said Martha. "You have a special gift that enables you to sense when things are not quite right. You are a true problem solver."

That the woman had such faith in my sleuthing abilities was both flattering and scary.

"It will be like you Americans say," Martha continued with a confident smile, "one hand will wash the other. It'll be our secret. Together, we will put our husbands on the road to health and happiness. Is it a deal?"

"But, Martha," I protested, "what happens if I fail? Or even worse, Matt finds out about my part in the plan?" In my head I could hear Matt's voice reminding me that he was the detective and I was the decorator. I was to stick with what I do best and he would do the same. "Everyone knows how he feels about me sticking my nose in police business."

"No, no, no. These things will not happen," Martha quickly replied. "Your birthday and mine are the same. Those who are born under the sign of Capricorn do not accept failure. Don't be concerned with your son-in-law finding out. He and Sergeant Rosen are far too busy with what Rollie tells me is an important investigation. Very hush-hush."

Rollie's assessment of Matt's involvement in an unrelated investigation jived with what JR had said when I'd asked for Matt's help. It also reminded me of something else my daughter had said in that same conversation: This time I was on my own.

"Okay, Martha, it's a deal," I said with more bravado than I actually felt. Only time would tell if the deal I agreed to would lead me back to the sunny side of the street or down a dark and dangerous path.

CHAPTER TEN

It was close to ten p.m. when I left Charlie in the capable hands of hospital personnel and called it a day. And what a day it had been. As I drove the short distance from the hospital to Kettle Cottage, I began to prioritize the things I needed to do to get my investigation of Dona's murder off the ground. Topping the list was verifying the time and cause of death. Obviously, a visit with Dr. Loo was in order.

I also needed to have a talk with Abner Wilson. If the old man who rented the cottage's barn and shed from Dona had been in the vicinity around the time of the murder, he might have seen or heard something of importance. And I wanted to interview the members of Dona's entourage, starting with Rufus Halsted. If the Deville/Halsted divorce was as acrimonious as Dona's personal assistant, Marsha Gooding, implied, then why was the ex a member of this select group? There must have been a pretty good reason. That the gossipy Goody had purposely misled me crossed my mind.

I hadn't a clue as to which one of the many bed-and-breakfast establishments in the Seville area counted the entourage among its guests. The thought of methodically checking out so many people, places, and things drained what was left of my energy. Maybe, I reasoned, what I really needed was some comfort food, a hot shower, and a good night's sleep.

Turning the van onto Blueberry Lane, I was surprised to find the normally dark road bathed in streams of light coming from the Birdwell house.

Separated from Kettle Cottage by a tall, thick hedge, the 1950s, five-bedroom, two-bath, brick Georgian was usually closed up for the night once the sun set. Its owner, Sally Birdwell, a perky forty-five-year-old widow, almost religiously adheres to the old adage of early to bed and early to rise. Knowing this, and that Billy Birdwell, Sally's twenty-two-year-old son, who was the assistant chef at the country club, generally didn't arrive home before midnight, I worried that Sally might have had some sort of mishap and was in need of help.

Before checking on my neighbor's well-being, I unlocked the back door of Kettle Cottage and checked on Pesty's. The little Kees had spent most of the day cooped up in the van, so when Mary had offered to dog-sit, I had happily given my consent.

As promised, Denny and Mary had dropped Pesty off after their dinner date with JR and the twins. Reeking of garlic bread, Italian meatballs, and tomato sauce, the little fuzz ball barely acknowledged my presence before resuming her late-night nap under the kitchen's round oak table.

"Don't bother getting up," I remarked as I deposited my purse and car keys on the countertop. "I know you're not really interested, but I need to run over to the Birdwells'. If I'm not back in an hour, you'll find a supply of dog treats in the pantry cabinet." When the sleepy pooch failed to respond to the word "treats," I made a mental note to speak to JR about overfeeding a certain four-legged family member who, unlike my daughter, was not eating for two.

Picking my way carefully through the prickly shrubbery and onto the small porch, I could see that almost all the lights in the Birdwell house had been extinguished. I was about to chalk the entire matter up to an overreaction on my part when the front door flew open and I found myself face to face with a sinister looking man. Somewhat portly, he was clad in a dark silk monogrammed robe and pajamas.

"Listen, sister," he growled, "like I told that other broad, I ain't got nothin' to say about Dona gettin' bumped off and neither does my kid, Ellie. Ya better vamoose before I call the cops."

"Mr. Halsted, would you please lower your voice. I'm afraid you'll wake up the others," scolded Sally Birdwell, pushing herself past the man and into the doorway. "I . . . oh my. Jean dear, is something wrong?"

"I was about to ask you the same thing," I replied, hiding my surprise upon learning that my verbal attacker was none other than Dona Deville's former husband, Rufus Halsted. "I saw all the lights on in your house and thought that perhaps you had a problem. I didn't know that you were entertaining overnight company."

"Hey, we ain't company," said Dona's ex, thrusting his swarthy face over Sally's shoulder, "we're payin' guests. Miz Birdwell promised Maxine that nobody would bother us at this here inn, 'specially nosy reporters."

"Mr. Halsted, this lady is not a member

of the press. If you must know," Sally said, "Jean is both a friend and neighbor who was concerned enough about my welfare to come over here and check on me. I suggest that you apologize to her before returning to your room. Sunday breakfast will be at nine a.m. sharp."

Rufus Halsted mumbled something that might have been an apology of sorts before disappearing into the house.

"Honestly, that man is impossible. I've repeatedly asked him not to answer the door or the phone, but . . ." Sally's voice trailed off as she brushed away an angry tear with the back of her freckled hand. "I never dreamed that running a bed-and-breakfast could be so difficult. It's like sharing your home with exiled royalty. No matter how nice you make things for them," she said, tucking a stray lock of her fiery, ginger-colored hair behind her right ear, "they never fail to remind you that they're used to better. This whole B-and-B business may be a one-time thing, but as far as I'm concerned, it's one time too many. This is all Hilly Murrow's fault."

"And why is that," I said, "if you don't mind my asking." Perhaps it was the lateness of the hour, coupled with the events of the day, but for the life of me I couldn't connect the dots.

"Because the whole thing was her idea," replied Sally, looking more pooped than perky. "Not only is she my closest and best friend, she's also my first cousin. When she asked me to help her out of a bind, naturally I said yes. It's times like this that I really miss my late husband. Fred always said Hilly took advantage of me, but I never believed it until now."

Fearing more tears, I fished a fresh tissue from the pocket of my blue jeans and passed it to Sally. "You were saying," I prompted.

"Oh dear, now where was I?" she asked before answering her own question. "Tuesday. It started that afternoon when Hilly phoned me in a dither," said Sally with a snort. "I should have suspected she was up to something 'cause she sounded so sweet. I don't know if you've ever noticed, but sometimes Hilly can be a bit abrasive."

Eager to hear more, I bit my tongue and shrugged my shoulders, hoping Sally would continue with her explanation, which she did.

"Hilly said that she owed someone a huge favor and that the person was pressing her for repayment. She made it seem as though it was a matter of life or death, so of course I told her I would help her out. I thought she needed money but it turned out that she needed my house! By the time I learned the truth, it was too late to back out."

"Wait a minute, Sally, let me get this straight. Hilly owed somebody a tremendous favor and she repaid the favor by turning your house into an instant bed-and-breakfast? That doesn't make a heck of a lot of sense. Why don't you start at the beginning and tell me the whole story."

"I guess I might as well," Sally said, pressing her lips into a tight line, "seeing that Hilly is too busy reporting on the murder to even answer my phone calls. But you must promise me you won't repeat what I tell you to anyone. Even though she pulled a fast one on me, Hilly's still family."

I gave Sally my word that I wouldn't tell a living soul and then listened while Sally told the tale of an ill-conceived friendship that had gone from bad to worse.

It all began years ago when Hilly was attending Northwestern University in Evanston, Illinois. She shared a small apartment with a fellow student, Maxine Roberts. Both were majoring in journalism, guys, and drugs. The apartment was known around the campus as party central. Eventually, someone tipped off the police. When the place was raided, Hilly wasn't there but

Maxine was, along with some cocaine. Maxine took the fall while Hilly went on to graduate with honors. Unlike Hilly, who quickly landed the job as Seville's radio and print reporter for the *Seville Sentinel,* our town's daily newspaper, Maxine Roberts spent years rebuilding her personal reputation while trying to get her professional career off the ground.

Five years ago, as a struggling press agent with a flair for creating good publicity for her clients, some of whom were not exactly model citizens, Maxine came to the attention of Dona Deville. She was hired as the health spa diva's public relations person. In spite of finally hitting it big, Maxine never forgave or forgot her former friend, Hilly Murrow.

"The way Maxine sees it," said Sally, "Hilly owed her then and still does. Maxine called her on Tuesday, demanding that Hilly find a nice, private place for Dona and her people to stay. Hilly promised me that they'd be be here for only two nights — last night and tonight. She said they'd be long gone by early Sunday morning. Of course, Dona's murder changed everything. I'm afraid that I'm stuck playing innkeeper for the six of them for God only knows how long."

I did some fast math in my head. With Dona out of the picture, the number of guests should have dropped to five. Had Sally made a simple error?

"Did you say six?" I asked, giving Sally the chance to correct her mistake.

"That's what I said, six," she replied with a sigh. "Shortly after what I thought was the entire group arrived last night, Mr. Salerno showed up on my doorstep claiming to be Ellie Halsted's bodyguard. After checking with Dona and finding that it was the case, I added him to the guest list. I figured what the heck — the more the merrier, Boy, was I wrong." Sally's usual upbeat disposition had all but disappeared. "If only Billy were here, then maybe I wouldn't feel so outnumbered, but he's staying at his girlfriend Tammie's place until these people clear out. I don't know when that's going to happen, but it can't be soon enough for me. What do you think I should do?"

"Well," I said, "I'm guessing that your guests are as anxious to leave as you are to see them go. Just be patient. Once Chief Stevens gives the okay, I imagine they won't waste any time getting out of town." I didn't add that I hoped to interview them while they were still within easy reach.

Unfortunately, I hadn't a clue as to how I

was going to accomplish this without being obvious. After my run-in with Rufus Halsted, I could hardly pass myself off as Sally's parlor maid or long-lost sister. "Just be patient," I repeated, "it'll all work out somehow." My advice covered Sally's situation as well as my own.

"I know you're right, Jean, but I can't help dreading breakfast time. These people make me feel as though I'm an interloper at my own table. Wait a minute," Sally exclaimed with a sudden burst of enthusiasm, "I've got a great idea. Why don't you join us? Then I'd have someone on my side, if you know what I mean. It's a serve-yourself buffet and I've got more than enough food. Please say you will. It would really mean a lot to me."

I could hardly believe my ears. Or my luck. With a hug and promise that I would join her and the guests for breakfast, I bid Sally a good night and made my way back to Kettle Cottage.

"And some people say that there's no such thing as the luck of the Irish," I remarked to Pesty as we shared a late-night snack of soda bread, cream cheese, and blueberry jam.

Later, climbing into bed, I recalled the words of the ultimate survivor, Margaret

Mitchell's Scarlett O'Hara, who, when confronted with the final adversity in *Gone with the Wind,* proclaimed that tomorrow was another day.

While visions of a hot-blooded, puffy-shirted Charlie toting me up an immense staircase passed before my tired eyes, I fell into a deep sleep. I'd had a day that even Scarlett would have found exhausting.

Chapter Eleven

Sunday morning arrived on the scene with blue skies and sunshine to spare. As expected, the weather forecast included record-high humidity, which meant it would be another hot and sticky summer day. With this in mind, I decided that my embroidered peasant blouse and skirt would be a wise choice. I pulled the gauzy, turquoise outfit from the laundry chute and tossed it into the recently repaired washing machine. Setting the timer on the quick, gentle cycle and the water on warm, I added a healthy squirt of detergent to the small load. Leaving the washer to do its thing, I headed for the kitchen and some coffee.

With a firm grip on a mug of instant, microwaved coffee, I used my free hand to unlatch the top half of the Dutch door and pushed it open. Leaning on the sill, I took a deep breath of fresh morning air. Resisting the urge to break into my own off-key version of "Oh, What a Beautiful Morning," I became aware of snippets of conversation coming from the direction of the Birdwells' backyard.

Still dressed in my nightshirt, I slipped out of the house and made my way over to the tall, thick, property-dividing hedge. Feeling more like a nosy neighbor than a fact-gathering sleuth, I waited for the conversation to continue. Judging from the pauses and hearing only one voice, I guessed correctly that I was eavesdropping on someone's cell phone call.

"Murdered. Yeah, like I told you before, it pays to be thorough. Let's just say, everything's turning out the way we expected. No, don't call me, I'll call you. It's safer that way. Ciao!"

The surreptitious conversation had come to an end. I'd certainly gotten an earful, but of what? The only thing I knew for sure was that the speaker was a man. The way things were going, it looked as though I would have more on my plate that morning than Sally Birdwell's breakfast fare.

Returning to Kettle Cottage, I decided to give Charlie a call while my clothes were in the dryer. I was pleasantly surprised when he picked up the phone on the first ring.

"Hi, sweetheart, I figured you'd be calling

me about now. How's my girl?" he asked, his voice thick with concern.

"Let's just say that she's doing a lot better today than yesterday, that's for sure." I didn't elaborate, which was just as well since it turned out my husband's inquiry pertained to Pesty and not yours truly. When I realized this, along with the fact that Charlie was unaware of what had taken place the previous morning out on Old Railway Road, I prudently ignored the faux pas.

"Hang on a minute, sweetheart. My breakfast tray just arrived," Charlie informed me. Judging from his less-than-stellar assessment of its contents, I knew then that my husband was on the road to recovery. As my Irish mother, Annie Kelly, would say, if you have the strength to complain, then you have the strength to endure. If nothing else, Charlie's tray tirade marked him as a complainer who would live to fight another day. The deal I'd made with Martha Stevens was looking better by the minute.

CHAPTER TWELVE

I arrived at the kitchen door of the Birdwell residence a good twenty minutes early, thinking my hostess probably was in need of an extra pair of hands and hoping to run into the cell phone talker. While not known for my culinary skills, I figured I could flip a couple of pancakes or perform some other mundane chore while Sally bustled to and fro setting up a modest buffet for her paying guests. Wrong.

After ushering me into the peach-, brown-, and cream-colored kitchen, complete with stainless-steel appliances, black granite countertops, buttery maple cabinetry, and terra-cotta tile floor, I was given a cup of freshly brewed, vanilla-flavored coffee, courtesy of Tammie, Billy Birdwell's girlfriend and coworker at the country club.

I watched in awe as Billy and Tammie quickly transferred pans of eggs Benedict, bacon-and-cheese omelets, fruit-laden crepes, and an assortment of homemade muffins from kitchen to dining room. While Sally set out her best china, the young couple went about arranging the various offerings on top of a highly polished console.

The large cabinet was part of the Queen Anne-style dining room suite. A round, white-framed mirror sat directly above the console and was flanked by a pair of black wrought-iron wall sconces. The lilac-gray-painted walls called attention to the room's white crown molding, and both were complemented by the pepper-and-salt chenille upholstered dining chairs.

Charcoal-gray carpeting, pearl-gray plantation shutters, a smoke-gray glass-and-brass chandelier, and white-trimmed, lilac-gray-painted French doors leading to an outside redwood deck completed the room's monochromatic color scheme.

A fresh floral arrangement of purple cornflowers, yellow black-eyed Susans, and delicate lady fern added a splash of unexpected color to the white-lace-covered table. The floral centerpiece was the perfect finishing touch to the formal but inviting space. The homeowner's good taste was reflected in the overall decor. I half expected to find Beaver's father, Ward Cleaver, seated at the head of the table.

"Isn't it wonderful," cooed Sally with a smile that spread across her pleasant face, causing her green eyes to crinkle. "Having a son who's also a chef. Of course, Tammie being a top-notch waitress certainly makes things even easier. And to think that I'm their very first customer."

"Slow down, Sally. You lost me somewhere between chef and customer. What's going on?"

"Oh sorry, Mrs. Hastings. We thought for sure that you heard about my plans to start a catering service," interjected Billy, handing Tammie the last of the items for the buffet. "In a town the size of Seville, news travels fast. But I guess the bad news of Dona Deville's murder beat out my good news. Gossip has it that Chief Stevens is handling the investigation and not Lieutenant Cusak. Is that true?"

Since I wasn't at liberty to explain why this was so, I merely nodded my head. Tammie's announcement that the guests were beginning to gather in the living room saved me from any further questions regarding the unusual situation.

"Okay, Mom, I think you and Mrs. Hastings will be able to manage things here. Tammie and I need to get back to her place and put her kitchen back together," said a grinning Billy.

"That's for sure," teased Tammie, playfully shoving Billy out the back door. "And this time, mister, you wash and I wipe. Later, Mrs. B., and you, too, Mrs. H."

Once we'd said our good-byes to the young couple, Sally decided that the time had come to introduce me to the guests.

"Hold it," she cried, removing the chef apron and smoothing out the folds of her pale green, A-line linen dress, "I'll be darned if I'm going to look like the hired help in my own home. Okay, now I'm ready. Come on, Jean, let's knock 'em dead."

In view of the fact that I was on Chief Stevens's short list of murder suspects, I felt Sally's phrasing left something to be desired. With my own list of suspects still forming in my head, and with my heart in my mouth, I followed Sally down the short corridor that led from the kitchen, past the dining room, and into the formal living room.

CHAPTER THIRTEEN

"Hastings you say. Would that be Jean Hastings as in Designer Jeans, the interior design firm? Dona was really looking forward to having the cottage redone. She had some truly fabulous changes in mind for the old place."

I was about to answer when a tall, willowy, brown-eyed redhead with a picture-perfect face and figure sauntered into the small but cozy beige-and-rose-colored living room. "Good lord, Goody, Dona's been murdered and you want to discuss decorating ideas? Give it a rest."

"I suppose you're right, Maxine. I guess the reality of Dona's death, especially the murder part, hasn't quite sunk in yet. To do something like that, the killer must have been filled with hate." Goody sounded sadder than she appeared.

"Or fear. Maybe even love," said Maxine, looking around the room before zeroing in on Todd Masters, Dona's personal trainer, and according to Goody, her latest love interest. "How about it, Todd, would you kill for love?"

"Aren't you asking the wrong person?" replied Todd, his handsome face dark with anger. "If I remember right, I was told a few nights ago that I was incapable of loving anyone. The point was emphasized by the glass of wine thrown at me. Luckily, the glass is as replaceable as the person who threw it."

Everyone in the room was staring at Maxine Roberts, whose beautiful face had turned as red as her hair.

"Hey, knock it off," barked Ruffy Halsted, shoving a sheaf of papers into the battered briefcase he'd placed on a nearby walnut chair-side table. "The only one who cared about what was goin' on between you two and the sheets was Dona and she's dead. Pick somethin' else to talk about."

"You mean like which one of us was stupid enough to kill the goose that laid the golden eggs?" said Goody with a wicked smile. "I do hope our alibis for Saturday morning hold up under police scrutiny, don't you?"

The questions posed by the woman with the closely cropped brown hair and athletic physique hung in the air like so much chimney soot before being dispersed by the tinkling sound of a small, porcelain bell. The ringing of the bell was Sally Birdwell's polite way of announcing that the Sunday breafast buffet was ready.

Although it came as no surprise to me that Ruffy Halsted didn't adhere to the practice of women and children first, I was somewhat taken aback by Todd Masters's eagerness to reach the buffet ahead of Goody, Maxine, Sally, and me. Ellie Halsted and her bodyguard had yet to make their appearance.

I watched as the blond Adonis heaped enough food on his plate to feed a small army, or a certain little Keeshond, before plunking his muscle-bound body down in the nearest chair.

"Now that Dona's gone to that big health spa in the sky," Todd remarked to no one in particular, "maybe we can all go back to eating real food and not that crap she peddled."

"And that's the truth," Sally whispered to me. "I'll tell you later about Saturday's breakfast. Believe me, it was nothing like this."

From the way his fellow guests attacked the contents of the buffet, it was obvious that they agreed with Todd Masters's assessment of Dona's line of expensive health food products. Once seated at the table, the feeding frenzy began. When it finally subsided, Marsha Gooding once again brought up the subject of alibis.

"The way I figure it," said Todd, flashing a dazzling smile, "Dona was murdered sometime after leaving here at a few minutes past seven and when the body was found at nine thirty yesterday morning. Since none of us left the house until at least eight o'clock, we only need alibis that cover an eight to nine thirty timeline, which is exactly when I happened to be jogging in the park. I don't know about the rest of you, but my alibi is as simple as it is solid."

"Your alibi is about as simple as you are, buddy boy, and it's about as solid as dog pee. Who's gonna swear to it that you were in the park? Name me one person," challenged Ruffy.

"I can't but I'm sure when the police chief checks it out, he'll find plenty of people who'll remember seeing me at that time," said Todd. Then he added, "I don't imagine the local yokels in this town see a well-toned, muscular body like mine very often, so it follows that they'll remember the 'bod' even if they can't recall the face."

I immediately thought of half a dozen

young men in Seville, all of whom were built as well or better than the conceited personal trainer, including Billy Birdwell. But anxious to hear more, I let it pass without comment.

"I can do you one better when it comes to an alibi," said Goody, sipping from a seemingly bottomless mug of herbal tea. "I arrived at the Book Nook a few minutes after eight o'clock yesterday morning and didn't leave there until after ten. Maxine saw me there. Isn't that right, Maxine?"

Instead of answering in the affirmative, Maxine Roberts shook her her head, "Listen, Goody, let's get something straight. I drove over to the Book Nook by myself as did you, sweetie. When I arrived, there was a sizable crowd waiting to get in and the store manager jumped the gun. He opened the doors at eight instead of nine and the people flooded in. I was busy setting things up for the book-signing gig, which included photo ops and interviews. With all that and the crowd, I didn't keep tabs on when you came and went."

"So what are you saying, Maxine?" asked Goody in a most unpleasant voice. "That I killed Dona, then drove over to the Book Nook to establish an alibi? Or maybe you think that I sneaked out of the store, murdered Dona, and then sneaked back in again?"

"I'm not saying anything of the kind but you have to admit, either scenario is a possibility." The gorgeous redhead helped herself to a biscuit, strawberry jam, and another cup of coffee. "In view of the scenarios that you just suggested, I'd be a fool to jeopardize my rock solid alibi by validating your rather questionable one. No way, no how, sweetie."

Goody was visibly shaken. For a moment there, I thought she might bolt from the room. Instead, she shifted the attention away from herself and onto Rufus Halsted.

"How about you, Ruffy? I know you had the motive to do the crime, so did you also have the time?" Goody had gotten her groove back. She even managed another sly smile.

"Hey, stuff it, Goody. I slept in yesterday mornin' 'til ten, just ask Miz Birdwell." Rufus Halsted's eyes had narrowed into snake-like slits. "And don't give me that motive crap. Every one of us, 'cept maybe Ellie, had a reason for wantin' Dona dead," he hissed, "including Salerno, the bodyguard. I wonder what the hell his alibi is because he wasn't with the kid. Ellie told me that when she went for a walk after breakfast yesterday,

113

she didn't see him or his car, ain't that right, Miz Birdwell?"

"Really, Mr. Halsted, I was rather busy in the dining room, so I couldn't say who did what, when, where, or even with whom. Now, if you will excuse me, I have to check on something in the kitchen. Jean dear, would you give me a hand?"

Once Sally and I reached the kitchen, she motioned to me to close the door between the two rooms. Then, following her lead, I stepped into the walk-in pantry.

"Good, nobody will hear us in here," said Sally. "Let me tell you about yesterday's breakfast. It was a fiasco with a capital F."

"Okay, Sally, I'm all ears. What happened? Talk fast. I don't think it'll look good if we're away too long." I didn't mention that I also didn't want to miss anything.

"First off, I tried to make a nice breakfast, although it certainly wasn't as grand as the one today, but then I'm not a professional chef like my Billy."

I nodded my head impatiently. "Hey, if you were, Pesty would be your new best friend." The pantry was getting stuffy. It had a faint onion odor that Sally either didn't notice or chose to ignore. "Now, tell me what happened."

"It started at about seven on Saturday

morning," Sally began, "with Dona walking into the dining room and finding that all her people were still in their rooms. She dashed upstairs and pounded on the doors, shouting that they had five minutes to get downstairs for breakfast or — and these are her words, not mine — she would kick ass and replace the freakin' lot of them with people who would abide by her rules.

"Everybody but Mr. Halsted came running downstairs and into the dining room. They began filling their plates with those nice little microwave and toaster breakfasts. I probably should have cooked from scratch but there simply wasn't time. Dona took one look at what they were about to eat and screamed that they were going to contaminate their bodies with useless carbs, empty calories, and bad cholesterol. Then she dumped all the food on the floor and put a big jar of pills, along with sticks of what looked and smelled like moldy bird food, in the middle of the table."

"Let me guess," I said, interrupting Sally's recap of the event, "the pills and smelly sticks were part of what Todd Masters poetically referred to as the crap that Donna peddled."

"Exactly," Sally said, bobbing her head in agreement. The movement allowed a ringlet to escape from the pale green scrunchy that encircled an almost picture-perfect chignon.

"Then Dona stormed out of the house shouting that there was one more thing that she had to take care of before — again these are her words — the freakin' sideshow at the Goddamn Book Nook. By the time I'd finished cleaning up the mess, it was after eight and everyone had gone out except Mr. Halsted. He says he slept 'til ten but how would I know?"

"Listen, Sally, I think maybe it's time that I level with you. What I'm about to admit to you mustn't be repeated to anybody, not even Billy."

"Don't tell me — you killed Dona Deville! You didn't, did you?" The prim and proper widow looked mortified. "How much does Charlie know?"

"In answer to your questions — no, I didn't kill Dona and Charlie doesn't know anything. He's in Garrison General with a broken kneecap."

"Oh, you poor thing. Why didn't you tell me this last night? I never would have insisted on your coming over this morning to help me out."

I purposely ignored her response. "Sally, what I've been trying to tell you is that I'm conducting a secret investigation into the murder at the request of someone. It's a someone who has asked that their name be kept out of it."

"My goodness, and here I thought the murder was making my life more complicated. What can I do to help?"

"Well, for starters, get us out of this pantry and back to the dining room before we both end up smelling like leftover chip dip."

"Of course," said Sally. "Gee, this is exciting. You probably want to grill the suspects or whatever it is you need to do." Giving me an unexpected hug, she added, "I'm so relieved that you're not the murderer. Think how embarrassing that would have been for your family."

Once back in the dining room, I'd just poured myself a needed cup of fresh coffee when Ellie Halsted, along with the bodyguard, entered the room. Sally, the perfect hostess, graciously handled the introductions.

The twentysomething girl's coloring favored her father rather than her mother. She had jet-black hair, dark eyes, and an olive complexion. Her height, like her weight and facial features, was in the average range. But there was nothing average about her megawatt smile or the deep dimples that accompanied it. This was the same smile that helped propel her mother, Dona, from local cutie to celebrity beauty.

As with the subject of the Deville/Halsted divorce, I found myself questioning comments made by Marsha Gooding regarding Ellie Halsted and the apple falling far from the tree and out of the orchard.

CHAPTER FOURTEEN

"Just call me Vinny and I'll call you Jean," announced the stocky man with the shaved head. His brown eyes squinted in a futile effort to block the smoke produced by the cigarette that dangled from the side of his turned-down mouth.

I'd taken what I thought would be an opportunity to go one-on-one with the bodyguard when I followed him out to the redwood deck. Being the only other smoker among the guests, the likelihood was practically nil that anyone would join us in the designated smoking area. But before I could stick my nose in his business, I found myself outmaneuvered.

"Word has it, Jean, that you're a talented interior designer. I understand your daughter, Lieutenant Cusak's wife, is a junior partner in Designer Jeans, the decorating service you operate out of your place here on Blueberry Lane."

The man's rapid-fire delivery, along with his knowledge of me and mine, caught me by surprise. It wasn't easy but I made an effort not to let it show, although the same could not be said of my growing irritation.

"Maybe you and your daughter should consider yourselves lucky that the cottage job fell through."

"Oh really? Would you care to explain that to me, chum?" I shot back, taking advantage of a pause in the so far one-sided conversation. The pause occurred when the bodyguard stopped talking long enough to take a deep drag on his cigarette.

"Sure, no problem. Old places like that cottage can be hazardous to your health. Look what happened to Dona Deville."

Not sure if I'd just been warned or threatened, I was determined not to let the beefy bozo think that he had frightened me. "Hey, chum, like they say, nobody lives forever."

"Yeah, so I hear. I also hear that you fancy yourself to be a detective of sorts. Take it from me, Jean, stick to decorating. Not only is it healthier but it pays better, too."

The man's smile was about as sincere as the overused, seldom-meant "have a nice day" tagline.

More angry than frightened, I decided it was time to find out if Mr. Salerno could take as well as he gave. I proceeded to hit him with what I hoped were probing questions. To my frustration, he ignored most of them and the few he didn't, he answered with about as much candor as the Nixon White House displayed during the dark days of Watergate.

Ask a stupid question and you get a stupid answer, which is what happened when I pressed the bodyguard for his alibi.

"My alibi? No problem," said the cagey guy. Finished with his cigarette, he quickly lit another. "My horoscope said that I should watch for signs of change so Saturday morning I got in my car and went looking for them."

"You don't say! Was that before or after the dog ate your homework? You're going to have to do better than that, if not with me, then with the people in there," I replied, jabbing my thumb in the direction of the dining room, "and certainly with the police." If the last part of my comment bothered him, he hid it well.

In the end, about all I did learn was that he, Salerno, had been hired by Dona as Ellie's bodyguard shortly after the death of Dona's elderly aunt. When Ruffy insisted on driving Ellie to Seville, minus the bodyguard, Dona gave the okay with the stipulation that Salerno was to be at the Birdwell house no later than eight o'clock Friday night. According to him, Ruffy's purpose for being alone with Ellie was to enlist her aid in convincing Dona to sell off some property that was jointly owned by Ruffy and his former wife.

I felt much of the information I'd gleaned from my conversation with the chain-smoking bodyguard was, both literally and figuratively, more smoke than substance. But I was firmly convinced that "Just call me Vinny" and the early-morning cell phone talker were one and the same.

Perhaps, I said to myself, my old friend Horatio Bordeaux would like to take a crack at getting the lowdown for me on the secretive Vincent Salerno. Horatio (a former CIA agent and retired professor of science) and I had become good friends when he hired Designer Jeans to transform his inefficient, drab home office into a cheery, modern, handicapped-accessible workplace. Suffering from diabetes, the rotund, wheelchair-bound widower started his own business on the web. His specialty is locating hard-to-find people, places, and things, including information, which is why I added his name to my growing lists of "must see" people.

I left the bodyguard in a cloud of his own

making, stubbed out my cigarette in a nearby sand-filled coffee can, and returned to the dining room. The once-bountiful buffet had been reduced to a few scraps and crumbs in the relatively short time I'd been out on the deck. Even the commercial-size coffee urn had been emptied.

Back among the less-than-grieving entourage, I came to the conclusion that when Hilly Murrow filed her report on the group's reaction to Dona Deville's murder, the newshound must have been on something stronger than baby aspirin. Either that or Maxine Roberts was one heck of a public relations person. My inherited Irish intuition told me that most likely, it was the latter rather than the former.

After helping Sally clean up the mess from the breakfast buffet, I returned to Kettle Cottage and the little Kees with the insatiable appetite.

CHAPTER FIFTEEN

"Listen, you bossy little ball of fur, lunch in this house isn't served until noon. You have to wait," I said to Pesty, who had dramatically draped herself over her empty food dish. "Go ahead and pout, but it won't do you any good."

Ignoring the dog, I fixed a cup of instant coffee, opened a package of snickerdoodles, and settled down at the kitchen table. I wanted — make that needed — a bit of time to relax and collect my thoughts before heading to the hospital for my afternoon visit with Charlie.

Despite Pesty's insistence that it was time for her lunch, I managed to concentrate long enough to review Vincent Salerno's alibi. The man didn't have a sense of humor, at least not that I'd noticed, so why the convoluted alibi? The more I thought about it, the more I was convinced that the body-guard had deliberately presented me with a puzzle within a puzzle. Did he really expect me to believe that he was following his horoscope and spent the time during which Dona was murdered looking for signs of change?

I put the alibi matter on hold and turned my thoughts to which member of the entourage had the best motive and, as Marsha Gooding so aptly put it, was stupid enought to kill the goose that laid the golden eggs.

"What Maxine said about killing out of fear or love, and what Goody said about killing out of hate, certainly gives me some food for thought," I said aloud, forgetting that Pesty was on the alert for certain trigger words such as eat, treat, and food. Upon hearing the word "food" the spoiled pooch positioned herself in front of me and began stamping her paws, something I've learned to recognize as her "chow now" dance. I've also learned to ignore it, but since a Pesty with a full tummy would, most likely, settle down for a nap, I gave in.

While Pesty dozed under the kitchen table, I composed a list of suspects along with possible motives for the murder:

NAME	HYPOTHETI-CAL MOTIVE
Rufus (Ruffy) Halsted	contentious property dispute
Ellie Halsted	hidden hostility
Marsha (Goody) Gooding	pent-up resentment
Todd Masters	unhappy with boy-toy role
Maxine Roberts	jealous of Dona/Todd twosome
Vincent Salerno	

Since I'd drawn a blank with Salerno's possible motive for the murder, I thought again about contacting Horatio Bordeaux to make arrangements for a complete background check on the bodyguard but decided to wait until Monday. The most important thing I wanted to do at that moment was to visit Charlie.

I had the keys to the van in my hand and was headed for the kitchen's Dutch door when the phone rang. Thinking it might be Charlie calling, I dropped everything and ran for the phone. Being that it was Sunday, I didn't bother with the usual Designer Jeans greeting, something which apparently flustered the caller.

"Is this Designer Jeans?" demanded the female voice with a barely perceptible Spanish accent. "Is that you, Jean?"

"Yes, Martha, it's me. Don't tell me that Charlie has been giving you a hard time already," I said, remembering his R-rated description of the breakfast tray's contents. As a rule, my husband is the most charming of fellows, that is unless he's hungry, tired, or incapacitated in any way, shape, or form.

"I didn't realize that his therapy would be starting so soon. There's nothing wrong, is there? I mean with Charlie?"

"No, no, no. I was in to see him after breakfast this morning and we hit it off like two old amigos. I know he appreciated the back rub and sponge bath I gave him. He called me an angel sent from heaven. He is so charming. You are a lucky woman to have such a man."

Relieved that my husband was doing fine, I sank down into the nearest chair and shakily lit a cigarette. "Yes, I am and he's a prince all right. But surely you didn't call me just to chat about Charlie's charm. If you're worried about my part of our bargain, I can honestly say that I've been working on it almost the entire morning."

I was about to fill her in on "Breakfast with the Suspects" when Martha hit me with the news that the medical examiner,

Dr. Loo, confirmed the police chief's belief that Dona Deville had been strangled to death sometime between seven thirty and nine thirty Saturday morning. While Loo's confirmation didn't surprise me, what Martha had to say next most certainly did.

"Dr. Loo told Rollie the marks on the victim's throat were made by the stethoscope found at the crime scene," said Martha. "I pray you will solve this murder before my Rollie does something foolish. I fear he's going to arrest the wrong person." The anxiety in Martha Stevens's voice was palpable.

Without mentioning the name, we both suspected that the wrong person in this case was Dr. Peter Parker. But you could never be sure about these things. It would take more investigating.

"I must go now, Jean, or I will be late for church. When mass is over, I will light a candle and ask the Virgin Mary to help you with your investigation."

"Thanks," I said, then added, "and would you do the same with Saint Jude? That way, we'll cover all the bases. Besides, I need all the help I can get." It was nice not having to explain my request further. Martha, a devout Catholic, was well aware that Saint Jude is the patron saint of hopeless causes.

Before leaving for my visit with Charlie, and with a truly heavy heart, I added the young doctor's name to my list of suspects along with the possible motive of revenge for the death of his anorexic fiancée. Considering Dr. Loo's findings, I probably should have told Martha to light every candle in the church and then some.

CHAPTER SIXTEEN

Charlie was lucky in that he didn't have to share his hospital room with another patient. The empty bed provided the extra seating needed for a small contingent of my husband's golf cronies. The foursome, along with Denny England, were supposedly visiting their good buddy, Charlie. Personally, I don't consider watching a televised rerun of last year's Masters Tournament (in virtual silence, mind you) visiting, but then I'm not a "real golfer."

"Mind if I play through?" I joked as I made my way over to Charlie's bedside. My attempt at humor was met by a string of shushing sounds. Not wanting to start off on a sour note, I smiled through gritted teeth, patted the top of Charlie's head, and dutifully sat down in the chair vacated by the gentlemanly Denny England.

After sitting through what seemed like a jillion shots of a jillion golfers at the tee, in the fairway, and on the green, I was resigned to the fact that Charlie and I were not going to have an in-depth conversation. While I had been prepared to give my husband an abridged version of Dona's murder that minimized my involvement in the aftermath, I wasn't prepared to do so in front of an audience of golf devotees. When a temporary halt in the action (an oxymoron in my opinion) was called, I bid adieu to Charlie and the golf gang and headed for the nearest exit, a cigarette, and some needed female company.

A couple of hours and phone calls later, I was sitting in Milano's sharing an extra-large, thin-crust Italian sausage pizza and a pitcher of fresh-squeezed lemonade with JR and Mary. For the time being, I put all thoughts of murder and mayhem out of my mind. Instead, I made a conscious effort to enjoy the meal, my companions, and the sunny side of the street.

"Matt finally took some time off. He and the twins went to Indianapolis to see a movie," JR said between bites of the delicious pizza. "Afterward, they're going to Pufferbelly's in the Circle Centre Mall. Ever since the twins ate there last fall, it's become their favorite downtown Indy restaurant. I'd love to see the look on Matt's face when his dinner arrives on a toy train."

"My stars, I swear no matter how old they are, all men are little boys at heart," Mary remarked as she poured herself a second glass of lemonade. "Watch, one visit to Pufferbelly's and he'll probably want a set of trains for his birthday."

"Oh great, that's just what I don't need — a fourth child." As soon as the words had popped out of her mouth, JR blushed and began to sputter before falling silent. For a moment or two even Mary was speechless.

Reaching across the table, I gave my daughter's hand an understanding pat. "I was wondering when you were going to say something about it. How far? About three months?"

JR smiled. "You got it. Why do I have this feeling that you're not exactly surprised? What tipped you off?"

"Let's just say that you can fool all the people some of the time but you can never fool your mother." I didn't see any reason to bring up my medicine cabinet discovery.

"Well, this isn't exactly how I planned on breaking the news. Matt and I haven't even told the twins yet. Until we do, I'm afraid that mum's the word."

"Whoa, wait just a minute," cried Mary, waving her hands in the air, "am I right in thinking that you two are talking about what I think you're talking about? Or am I talking about something entirely different than what you two are talking about?"

"Hey, Aunt Mary, if it's a girl, I'll name her after you, that is if you can repeat verbatim what you just said." JR's infectious giggle spread over the three of us like sauce on a pizza pie.

We were trying to compose ourselves when Angela, the restaurant's hostess, swept past our table as she led a young couple to a secluded corner where a table had been set for two. Although it was late in the afternoon, there was plenty of sunshine everywhere except in Milano's dining room.

The room's decor was basic 1970s Mediterranean with cherubic wall murals, rich velvety fabrics, heavily carved dark wood furniture, and overly ornate light fixtures with thick, colored-glass panels. The fixtures bathed the room and its occupants in a soft, romantic, candle-like glow. In spite of the dimness, I recognized the young Dr. Peter Parker and his date, Ellie Halsted.

Mary and JR also recognized the young doctor but were at a loss when it came to Ellie Halsted. They listened while I explained who she was and how I'd come to meet her and the rest of the Deville party.

I should have left it at that, but my ego got in the way of my good sense. I continued to babble on until Mary and JR knew as much about my investigation as I did. The only thing I left out was Martha Stevens's name and the details of our bargain. JR was the first to react.

"Thank God Matt has other fish to fry," she said, alluding to his involvement in an unrelated investigation, "otherwise I hate to think what he would do. At the very least, Mom, he'd put your name on his persona non grata list."

"My stars, is that legal? After all, your mother is a citizen of the United States," cried Mary, her voice crackling with concern.

"Don't worry about it, Mar. If I solve the case, I'm sure Matt will forgive me like he has in the past." I didn't bother to explain to Mary that I wasn't in danger of being bounced out of the country. In a way, Mary's interpretation of the phrase was pretty much on the money. I'm sure when the alleged Mafia big shot Lucky Luciano was deported by the feds, he felt like an outcast even though he ended up in the land of his birth.

"Okay, now comes the big question," I said, trying to look and sound more confident than needy. "Anybody here interested in helping a certain designing woman with an investigation that is in dire need of a makeover? If the answer is yes, the said designer will spring for dessert. Rumor has it that today they have Mama Milano's homemade baklava."

Faster than you can say Sam Spade, private investigator, Mary and JR were devouring huge portions of the melt-in-your-mouth nut-and-honey Mediterranean pastry. Meanwhile, Peter Parker and Ellie Halsted were enjoying the bottle of Chianti that Papa Milano delivered to their table with my compliments. My little wine investment paid off just as I'd hoped it would.

By the time the late-afternoon sun began to make way for the evening stars, we were sharing a large carafe of Milano's special-blend coffee and our table with Peter Parker and Ellie Halsted.

Chapter Seventeen

"I don't deny it. I was really angry with Dona Deville and blamed her for encouraging young women like Karen, my former fiancée, to be stick thin. She said terrible things in that stupid book of hers, *Be Thin and Win,* like overweight people are life's losers, and therefore in order to succeed in life, you must be thin . . ."

"And the thinner the better," said Ellie Halsted, finishing the young doctor's sentence. "In my mother's opinion, I was a failure, just like my father, and she never let me forget it."

Anxious to hear how Peter expressed his anger, I asked if he'd planned to confront the diet diva at the Book Nook's signing gig.

"No, not at all," he said in answer to my question. "That's what I'd planned to do the day I stormed into Dona's office several years ago. I'd just come from Karen's funeral service. I got about three words in before she had Todd Masters toss me out the front door. That's when I met Ellie. I was going out the door as she was going in. I can truly say that I knocked her off her feet, right, honey?"

"Right," Ellie said, smiling at the memory. "Of course, he had no idea that I was Dona's daughter and I had no idea why my mother had had him forcibly removed from the premises. But we sorted it all out over coffee later that month."

"Ellie listened while I dumped all the blame for Karen's death on Dona until I got around to realizing that I was really angry with Karen for being so foolish and with myself for not being able to save her."

"And we both knew that our first meeting wouldn't be our last. Your timing with the wine, Mrs. Hastings, was perfect. It arrived right after Peter popped the question," Ellie added, flashing her megawatt smile.

"Tell them what your answer was," said a beaming Peter Parker.

"I'll do better than that," replied Ellie, extending her left hand to show us the diamond engagement ring that she'd accepted from Peter along with his proposal of marriage.

The engagement news ended any discussion of Dona's murder, or so I thought until Mary, in her own flaky way, brought the matter to the forefront of discussion again.

"Oh my stars," gushed Mary. "I'm so happy for the two of you. Will the wedding take place here or in Indianapolis?" Not waiting for an answer, Mary plowed on, "It's a shame that Designer Jeans never had the chance to redo that old cottage. It would've been the perfect honeymoon hideaway or a fantastic starter house for a young couple such as yourselves."

"Aunt Mary," scolded JR, "are you forgetting what happened out on Old Railway Road last Saturday? I imagine Ellie would just like to forget everything and everybody connected with the cottage."

"No, as callous as it may sound, my mother's death wasn't exactly a big surprise, at least not to me." said Ellie. "The surprise was that she died the way she did. I thought for sure the end would come as a result of an overdose. She was really hooked on prescription drugs. My father and I tried to get her into rehab but she just blew us off, saying things like we were losers and that we were the ones who needed help."

Pausing for a moment to collect herself, Ellie then continued. She told of living with a mother whose physical appearance supposedly was the result of using the products and following the programs promoted by Dona's Den and the Dona Deville self-help books. But the diet diva never followed any of her own programs or used any of her own products. Instead, Dona turned to surgery and drugs to attain her goal of staying forever young and thin.

"People say that I don't look like my mother. Believe me, eventually even my mother didn't look like herself. You name the procedure and she'd had it done. The last straw, as far as my father was concerned, was when she had her stomach stapled at a time when she was already underweight."

"In other words, Ellie," said JR, "although your mother talked the talk, she didn't walk the walk."

"Exactly, but she had no compunction taking money from those who did. Don't get me wrong. My father and I loved my mother but we were saddened by what she'd become."

"And what was that?" Mary asked in a gentle voice and looking close to tears.

"A manipulative, power-hungry woman who cared more about herself and her wealth than the health of her followers," replied Ellie, her voice dropping to an almost inaudible whisper. "But she still was my mother and she never stopped worrying about me."

"Is that why she hired the mad joker to be your shadow? Incidentally, shouldn't he be lurking behind the drapes or the potted palms?" I was trying to play it light. I didn't want the girl to feel as though she was being interrogated.

"You mean Vincent? He's more like a big brother than a bodyguard," declared Ellie. "Mother hired him after Auntie died. She was convinced the death wasn't an accident. At one point, she started carrying a gun for protection. When I refused to do the same, she hired Vincent to watch over me even though she knew I was seeing Peter. Eventually, I got Vincent to back off a bit on the bodyguard stuff. I don't know where he is at the moment, do you, Peter?"

"Most likely, he's sitting in the bar watching TV," said the young doctor. "That's what he usually does when Ellie and I are out on a date. Do you want me to see if I can find him?" Ellie and I answered in unison with a resounding no.

With Frank Sinatra's rendition of "My Way" floating through the restaurant, courtesy of the jukebox, I silently vowed that with the help of JR and Mary, I would do everything to keep my part of the bargain

I'd made with Martha Stevens. I kept my fingers crossed that Saint Jude was listening when Martha was praying. Using all the tact I could muster, I pressed Peter for his alibi. He claimed that he was alone in his uncle's medical center office. He said he was catching up on paperwork. He saw no one nor did he make or receive any phone calls. My Irish intuition told me that Peter was innocent. It also told me that if Peter had committed the murder, he certainly wouldn't have been stupid enough to use his own stethoscope as the murder weapon. The murderer had probably deliberately used Peter's stethoscope in an effort to place the blame on the young doctor. All I had to figure out was who, when, why, and how did the murderer get his or her hands on the murder weapon.

CHAPTER EIGHTEEN

"My money's on that Goody woman," JR announced in a positive voice as she helped herself to a glass of milk and a toasted English muffin.

The milk and muffin were part of the modest breakfast I'd set out on the black granite countertop minutes before Mary and JR turned up at the back door of Kettle Cottage at nine o'clock Monday morning as promised. Mary had already filled her plate with a plump croissant, cream cheese, and blueberry jam and was waiting for JR to join us at the kitchen table.

"Let's not talk murder until after we've finished breakfast. By the way, Gin, is that all you're having? A cup of coffee? Don't tell me you're on a diet. You're not, are you?"

"Nope. If you must know, Pesty and I had scrambled eggs and sourdough toast an hour ago. When it comes to eating, Kees-

142

honds are like the time and tide — they wait for no man."

Before taking her seat at the table, JR poured a cup of coffee for Mary and topped off my cup. "There, now we're all set. Eat fast, Aunt Mary. I want to get to Mom's investigation stuff before I have to pick up the twins at the park's summer camp center. When I dropped them off, the bus driver said he'd bring the kids back by eleven."

"Back from where?" I asked, waiting for my coffee to cool and wishing I could have a cigarette. In view of JR's pregnancy, and the fact that there wasn't even a hint of a breeze coming through the open top half of the Dutch door, I put a lid on my wish for the time being.

"From a field trip," JR answered. "He's driving the camp kids out to the old railroad station. Can you believe it? The summer camp hasn't changed its curriculum in twenty-five years. I can still remember when I went out there as a summer camp kid. Mother was the bus monitor. Do you remember that day, Mom?"

"How could I forget it?" I replied, "I spent the hottest day of the year trapped on a non-air-conditioned bus with a certain fatheaded furniture salesman that we all know and love."

"Poor Mom," JR said, snatching a dollop of blueberry jam from Mary's plate and spreading it over what little remained of the English muffin. "She missed the whole tour of the place. The railroad station turned out to be a heck of a lot more interesting than most of the kids thought it would be. Sally Birdwell, I should say Sally Overbeck since she wasn't married then, gave the tour. Sally was about twenty at the time and all the young boys went gaga over her. I don't think they learned anything but we girls did. She told us about how important the station was before, during, and after the Civil War. There was even a picture of Lincoln standing on the station's platform when he was campaigning for the presidency."

"Overbeck, hmm. Isn't that the name of the Cambridge City sisters who made those whimsical figurines you've got in your bathroom, JR?" inquired Mary. Her cupid's bow lips were outlined in deep blue, courtesy of the jam that Mary had slathered over, in, and under the croissant.

"Same name but no relation. But Sally did tell us about the Overbeck kiln," said JR, handing Mary an extra napkin. "I can't remember what it was, but there was some kind of connection between the sisters, the railroad station, and the Civil War. Thanks to the tour and Sally, I developed an interest in Overbeck pottery. My collection of figurines is small but growing, kind of like me."

While JR and Mary laughed at JR's joke, I got up from my chair and retrieved the canister of towelettes that was sitting on the counter. If I had any hope of having a serious, in-depth discussion of my investigation and a review of my suspect list, Mary was going to have to ditch the blueberry lip liner.

"Here, try one of these," I said to Mary as I pulled a towelette through the asterisk-shaped opening on the canister's top, "before you draw blood with that paper napkin."

One swipe with the damp tissue and the stain was gone. With Mary once again looking like a beautiful, mature woman and not the bride of Frankenstein's monster, it was time to get down to business.

Taking a pad of yellow lined paper from my Designer Jeans briefcase, along with a couple of pencils and my list of suspects, I placed the writing materials and the list in the middle of the table. I then instructed JR and Mary to study my list before making a decision as to whom, in their opinion, was the most likely person to be the murderer. I suggested that they write down the suspect's name, motive, and means, and be ready to defend their decision. Thanks to my running off at the mouth when we were at Milano's the day before, Mary and JR were familiar with the members of Dona's entourage.

It didn't take either one of them very long. Mary was the first to finish. Holding up the sheet of paper and using the pencil as a pointer, she declared that in her opinion, Ruffy Halsted had murdered Dona.

"I feel that he had the motive and the means. I think he slipped out of his room, drove to the cottage, killed Dona, and then slipped back into his room with no one the wiser. His motive involved the real estate deal that someone, I think it was the bodyguard, had mentioned."

I could tell from the look on her face Mary was pleased with her decision and her reasoning.

"Sorry, Aunt Mary, I disagree. No way would he take such a chance. Someone could have checked his room, found him missing and then what? No alibi. Besides, how would he know where Dona was going when she stormed out of the house? He wasn't in the dining room at the time."

"If you take that one step further, JR," I interjected, "maybe nobody in the dining room knew where Dona was going or made any effort to follow her."

"Good point, Mom. That's why I ended up choosing Peter Parker and not Marsha Gooding or anyone else in the entourage. We only have his word that he no longer blamed Dona for Karen's death. Peter had the means — access to a stethoscope and his own car. He also doesn't have an alibi; at least not one that can be substantiated. I hate to say it but I think he's the one."

"My stars, I forgot all about the stethoscope," said Mary. "Maybe Ruffy Halsted used a stethoscope purposely to put the blame on poor Peter. That's a possibility to consider. Besides, how could Peter know that Dona would be at the cottage?"

"He probably contacted Dona the day before and set up an appointment to meet her there Saturday morning. What was it she said when she stormed out of the Birdwell house that morning?" asked JR, turning to me. "I've forgotten."

"Hold on while I check my notes," I replied. The two waited patiently while I dug further into my briefcase.

"Okay, I've got them. According to Sally Birdwell," I said, reading aloud from my notes, "Dona said something about having one more thing to take care of before going to the book signing gig at the Book Nook. To me, it sounds more like Dona was planning on doing the confronting rather than other way around. If Dona did have an appointment to meet someone at the cottage, I'm inclined to think that she was the one who set it up."

Pleased that JR and Mary agreed with my theory, I then moved on to the subject of Vincent Salerno and his puzzling alibi. The lengthy, unproductive discussion that followed only reinforced my desire to contact Horatio Bordeaux. I couldn't shake the feeling that the bodyguard and his alibi were key elements in the case. And the sooner the better or Ellie Halsted was in for a long engagement — like fifty years to life.

"Wow! Look at the time. I better get a move on if I'm going to pick up the twins. If I think of anything that might be of some help to you, even if it's trivial, I promise I'll call you on your cell, Mom, no matter what." That said, JR gave the lounging Pesty a final pat, her favorite aunt a hug, me a kiss, and headed out the Dutch door.

"My stars, this sleuthing business is a lot harder than I imagined," Mary remarked, helping herself to the last of the croissants. "Where do you want to go for lunch?"

CHAPTER NINETEEN

Mary had to settle for the hospital cafeteria. Unlike most people that I know who don't find institutional food all that great, Mary loves it. Pushing our trays along the stainless-steel counter that ran in front of a sea of unidentified entrees, vegetables, and the like, Mary made more stops than an overloaded school bus. By the time we'd reached the cashier, Mary's tray had become a burgeoning banquet of food while my tray looked rather forlorn.

"My stars, Gin. Are you sure you're not on a diet? What you've selected wouldn't satisfy a three-year-old much less a grown woman. At least go back and get yourself a dessert. Trust me, the bread pudding is to die for."

I thought about defending my choice of the cream of chicken soup, a small tossed salad, and an apple, but I didn't feel like it. Instead, I grabbed a dish of the mushy-looking pudding and stuck it on my tray, figuring that Mary would most likely end up eating the stuff. And why not, since she was picking up the tab for lunch. When the cashier rang up the bill for the two lunches, Mary paid while I went in search of a clean table for two. I was about to give up when I heard someone call my name. It was Dr. Sue Lin Loo and she was sitting alone at a table for four. Reading her hand signals, I then motioned to Mary that we would be sitting with the petite medical examiner.

After both the doctor and Mary had polished off their king-sized meals and were sipping diet soda, the conversation turned to the Deville matter.

"The body is being released Wednesday," Loo said between sips of soda. "From what I understand, Twall and Sons Mortuary will be handling the funeral."

"You sound surprised," I said, handing Mary the dish of bread pudding.

"To tell you the truth, I am. I thought for sure that her send-off would be held in Indianapolis. She certainly spent more time there than in Seville, but I guess her ex-husband and daughter want to bury her here, next to her aunt. By the way," said Loo, who had gotten up to leave, "it was Peter Parker's stethoscope that was found at the crime scene. I'm only telling you because for some reason, Rollie Stevens is handling the investigation and not Lieutenant Cusak. Don't get me wrong, I really like the chief, but when it comes to sorting out a complicated case, your record is better than Rollie's. It would be a shame if a certain young doctor's reputation ends up in shreds because of a bungled investigation."

"You got that right," I said, thinking of my own efforts, which so far had produced diddly-squat. I watched as Loo quickly walked out of the cafeteria without a backward glance.

"Come on, Mar, we got things to do and people to see," I said, collecting the dishes and trash from the table.

Mary's reaction was both predictable and immediate. "My stars, Gin. Now this is more like it."

"What's more like what? And for chrissake, stop calling me that idiotic name."

"More like real sleuthing," replied Mary, ignoring the admonishment. "What's the first thing on the list of things to do and who are we going to see?"

Mary's inner glow dimmed slightly when I informed her that while I was off to see Horatio, she would cover for me and visit

Charlie.

"What am I suppose to tell him when he asks why I'm there and you're not? You know I'm not good at telling lies like you are, Gin."

"Jeez, thanks for the left-handed compliment, Mar. I don't know. Tell him anything you want. Just don't tell him that I've gone to see Horatio. That would tip him off that I've got my nose stuck where it doesn't belong, at least in his and Matt's opinion. Now listen, Mary. This is really, really important. Find out how much Charlie knows about this whole Deville mess and my involvement in it."

Mary's face brightened considerably when I asked her to meet me at Kettle Cottage after her visit with Charlie. "If you're not too tired and if there's time, we'll drop in on Abner Wilson. If I'm not mistaken, his place is right off Fourth Street near the Sev-Vale college campus. And, Mary, there's one more thing I'd like to say before you go your way and I go mine."

"Okay, I'm listening," she said, looking so vulnerable that I felt even more guilty than I usually do after being short with her.

"I want to apologize for being so snippy. I guess my nerves are a bit frayed from everything that's happened. It doesn't help that my smoking has been cut down to the point that if I didn't know better, I'd think that old demon nicotine and I had parted ways." I was trying my damnedest to make amends to dear, sweet Mary. But like her twin brother, Charlie, Mary doesn't know when to quit.

"Oh, Gin, and here I thought you were crabby from dieting. Why didn't you tell me that you were trying to stop smoking? If you're not wearing a patch, you should be. You probably wouldn't be nearly so, you know, like edgy."

"Mary, do me a favor. I'm going to close my eyes and when I open them, you are going to be gone. You know what I'm saying?"

"Yes, I do and I forgive you. I guess your being hard is all part of being a good sleuth. I'll see you back at Kettle Cottage, Gin. Ta, ta."

When I opened my eyes, Mary was gone. I made a beeline for the parking lot, my van, and a cigarette.

CHAPTER TWENTY

"Yes, Mrs. Daggert, it's Jean Hastings. You know darn well who I am, and no, I am not wearing a disguise. My hair has always been this color, well, almost always, and these are precription sunglasses. Now let me in. I telephoned Mr. Bordeaux and he said it was okay for me to drop in on him. If you don't open the door right now, I'll tell your boss that you're up to your old trick of telling fortunes again. I'd like to see you talk your way out of that."

My threat worked. The massive front door slowly creaked open and I was ushered into the foyer by the eccentric housekeeper. Dressed from head to toe in black and with strands of colored beads in her stringy coal-black hair, on her neck, and around her waist, Lucrezia Daggert looked like a gypsy in search of a crystal ball.

"Wait here," she croaked, tottering off in the direction of Horatio's office. "And don't move 'til I tell you, otherwise you'll disturb the spell I put on you. I may be old but I still got the power."

Less than a minute later, I heard Horatio's deep laughter followed by Mrs. Daggert's announcement that Mr. Bordeaux would see me now.

"Come in and close the door," instructed Horatio. "That way we won't disturb Mrs. Daggert. She's recently taken up yoga and is into meditation."

"I think she's into more than that. If I were to guess, I'd say the cooking sherry. Why you put up with her, I'll never understand. I practically had to promise her my first born to get in to see you."

"Now, now, Jeannie, there's no need to exaggerate. I think your problems with Mrs. Daggert stem from your misinterpretation of her sense of humor," scolded Horatio with a twinkle in his eye.

"Okay, you win. The woman is a laugh a minute. Now that we've got that out of the way, I came to ask for your help in a very important matter."

"Why do I have this feeling that it has something to do with Dona Deville's murder," said Horatio as he maneuvered his wheelchair closer to his desk. "Fortunately, I've got a bit of free time on my hands so

I'm at your service. Why don't we start with you giving me a brief summary of the case as you see it so far. That way I'll have a better understanding of how I can be of help."

That's what I like about Horatio Bordeaux. He always cuts to the chase. With his unruly mop of salt-and-pepper curls, deep-set eyes, bushy beard, and wild taste in clothes, he has the look, and the credentials, of someone who has seen and done it all, from marching in 1963 with Martin Luther King Jr., to witnessing, firsthand, the 1989 destruction of the Berlin Wall. How he had time to party at Woodstock, ride horses in Ireland, and graduate with honors from Princeton is Horatio's secret.

An hour later, I was on my way to Kettle Cottage with Horatio's promise that he would get back to me ASAP with the background check on Vincent Salerno.

"I'm back," I called out to Pesty, who was tucked under the kitchen table. She had her head resting on one of Charlie's running shoes. Somehow she'd managed to get into the upstairs bedroom closet, find the shoe, and bring it down to the kitchen. For a dog who refuses to fetch any item that isn't edible, going through all that trouble demonstrated how much the little Kees missed her master.

Sitting down on the floor, I called her over and gave her some one-on-one attention. I also told her how much I missed Charlie. Putting our two heads together, we both cried until I heard the sound of Mary's car coming up the driveway.

"Come on Pesty, Aunt Mary's here." When the little ball of fluff failed to respond, I added, "You know, Pest, the lady with the purse-load of sugar cookies." Still nothing.

Dragging Charlie's shoe by the lace, Pesty crawled back under the round oak table. It was obvious to me that in Pesty's mind, if she couldn't have Charlie, then she would settle for the next best thing — something of his. In this case, it was his running shoe.

"It's okay, girl, I understand," I said to her as I gently pushed the shoe beneath her chin. "Maybe when I go to bed tonight, I'll try it your way. If it works for you, then maybe it'll work for me."

Mary plopped herself down in the nearest kitchen chair, kicked off her white sandals, and yanked her white denim skirt up past her dimpled knees. "Dear God, it must be at least a hundred degrees out there. I forgot to leave the windows of my car cracked open and when I got in it after visiting with Charlie, the seats were so hot that I thought I was going to melt. By the time the air-conditioning cooled the car down, I was pulling into your driveway."

"Hey, tell me about it. The AC in the van hasn't worked since Memorial Day. But you know what they say — it's not the heat, it's the humidity. Would you like a bottle of water or ice tea?" I asked, moving toward the refrigerator.

"I'll have what you're having," Mary replied, mopping her face with a white, lacy handkerchief, "that is, if it's not a cup of coffee and a cigarette. How you can do that when it's so hot is beyond me. That husband of yours is as bad as you are."

I was about to pour two glasses of lemonade to go with the cheese and crackers when I realized what Mary had said. "Charlie had coffee and a cigarette? I can't believe it. He hasn't had a cigarette in over a year. How could he do that in the hospital of all places? Like everywhere else in this town, Garrison General is a smoke-free zone."

"Who said anything about Charlie smoking? Honestly, Gin, sometimes you jump to the craziest conclusions. I only meant that Charlie had a cup of coffee when I was visiting him. One of his golf buddies brought a whole carryout container of mocha lattes from the Koffee Kabin."

"Golf buddies! Don't tell me, let me

guess. You spent the entire time watching golf on TV and never had a chance to talk to Charlie."

"My stars, how did you know? Denny was there, too. It wasn't all that bad. I managed to take a little nap between golfing bouts or whatever they're called. I woke up right in the middle of somebody getting a hole in one. The way everyone carried on, you would have thought it was like a home run or a touchdown."

"So what you're telling me is you never had a chance to say anything to Charlie or talk about the Deville case and see how much he knows about my involvement in it?"

"Yes and no. I did tell him about our stumbling on the body. I thought that was a nice way of putting it. He didn't seem very surprised. The only thing he asked was if you were upset about not getting the contract with Dona Deville. He never said anything about your being involved with the investigation. Apparently Martha Stevens, who seems to be in charge of Charlie's rehab and physical thereapy, told Charlie that her husband Rollie has everything under control."

"Well, that's a relief," I replied, lighting a cigarette. The last thing I needed was to have Charlie getting into a snit about my investigating Dona's death.

"Of course, he wanted to know where you were today so I said you had a really bad headache and asked me to visit in your place." Mary popped a cheese-topped cracker in her mouth and closed her eyes, savoring the blended flavors.

"And he bought that? He didn't have anything else to say?" Knowing Charlie as well as I do, I found it hard to believe that he fell for the old headache bit. I had to wait until Mary took another gulp of lemonade before she regained her power of speech.

"Nope, that was it. Oh, he did say something when I was leaving. He said to tell you that pretty is as pretty does and that includes noses. Pretty silly, huh?"

"Whatever," I replied. Well, at least I knew that he knew I'd stuck my nose into police business once again. Fortunately, thanks to the bee that stung Denny, my husband was not in any position to interfere in my ongoing investigation. But I also knew that I hadn't heard the last of it from my husband. The only bright cloud on the horizon was that Charlie was in no condition to retaliate and our son-in-law, Matt, was too busy with his own case to be bothered with the Deville murder.

"Come on, Mary, drink up. We still have time before dinner to drop by Abner Wilson's place. Last Saturday morning, he might have been out by the cottage doing what ever it is that he does with the equipment or painting stuff he keeps in the old barn and shed. It's possible he overheard or maybe saw something that might help solve the case."

"Okay, I'm done," said Mary, draining her glass of lemonade. "Your van or my car?"

"If you don't mind, let's take your car. Like I said, the AC in the van is on the fritz. I don't know if you're right about today's temperature, but it sure feels like it's a hundred degrees."

Reaching down to Pesty, I gave her a loving pat and a cracker loaded with cheese. I felt relieved to see that, in spite of her depression, she managed to eat the treat.

Once we were settled in Mary's car, I sat back and waited for the cool air to do its thing. We hadn't gone more than a couple of blocks when I knew the answer to the heat dilemma Mary encountered when she drove from the hospital to Kettle Cottage.

Drawing on my vast, unending supply of patience, I requested that Mary "turn off the bloody seat heaters," which she did. The rest of the short trip to Abner Wilson's house on Fourth Street was cool, quiet, and comfortable.

"We're in luck," I told Mary as we circled the block for the third time, "somebody up near the corner just pulled out. The space is big enough for a semi."

Since Mary doesn't exactly excel in parallel parking, she was relieved that, without any help from the two college boys who'd stopped to watch, she maneuvered the little PT Cruiser into the vacancy, leaving only a short walk from the car to the curb.

CHAPTER
TWENTY-ONE

With summer in full swing, there was a noticeable drop in the number of college kids in and around Seville. The few who remained all seemed to be living on Fourth Street. Situated between two Victorian-style fraternity houses was a nondescript brick two-flat. It was one of several that had been built in Seville during the early decades of the twentieth century.

Mary and I had positioned ourselves in front of the screen door and were patiently waiting for someone, anyone, to answer. There were two doorbells to choose from and both were marked with the name Wilson. I assumed that because of his age and gimpy leg, Abner would most likely live on the first floor, so I had pushed the lower bell. Thinking the old man might not have heard it, I gave it another, longer push.

"Yo, lady, give it a rest. My uncle ain't

home and I'm trying to cop some z's up here."

Looking up from the tiny square of cement that was more of a stoop than a porch, my gaze fell on a young man whose unkempt long hair hid his face as he leaned out over the waist-high, second-floor sill of the opened window. From my vantage point, he looked as though he wasn't wearing any clothes. It was only when he straighted up and turned away that I caught a glimpse of his low-riding jeans.

"Hey, come back here," I ordered the retreating figure. "Where's Mr. Wilson?"

The young man returned to the open window. "How the hell should I know? Do I look like his keeper?" he bellowed before disappearing from view.

If the twentysomething guy wasn't a drama student, he should have been. Mary agreed with me when I said if our local theater group ever decided to put on a production of Tennessee Williams's *A Streetcar Named Desire*, he would be perfect in the role of Stanley. I could almost hear his tortured and tortuous cry of "Stella!"

We were about to return to Mary's car when I caught sight of Abner Wilson's battered old truck turning the corner onto Fourth Street. I waved as he zipped past the house. He either didn't see me or was deliberately ignoring me.

With Mary close on my heels, I threaded my way through the backyard jungle of rusted car parts, plastic bags of empty aluminum cans, and the skeletal remains of an assortment of nonworking household appliances. When the elderly handyman, and I use the term loosely, brought the ancient pickup to a halt in the alley behind the Fourth Street house, Mary and I were on hand to greet him. It was something the old grouch didn't seem to appreciate.

"Hi there, Mr. Wilson," I called out to him in the most pleasant voice I could muster. "If you've got a minute to spare, I'd like to ask you a couple of questions." I followed the request with my best Doris Day smile.

The old man was having none of it. "Ain't you got somethin' better to do than bother me? Seems to me, you should be home where you belong and that goes for your friend, too. Women," he said as if it were a bad word. He emphasized his contempt by spitting out a mouthful of tobacco juice. The disgusting brown liquid landed about two inches from my open-toed shoes. "We shoulda never given you the vote."

It was clear to me that the cantankerous elderly man was doing his best to draw me into an argument. It wasn't easy, but I ignored his caustic comment and obnoxious behavior. Instead, I folded my arms across my chest, looked him in the eye, and asked him straight out if he'd been in the vincinity of the old cottage Saturday morning.

Squinting his eyes and rubbing his chin, he seemed to be giving my question some serious thought. "Last Saturday, you say? Nope, never went near the place. How come you're askin' me somethin' like that? What are you tryin' to do? Take over the police chief's job? I already told 'em I wasn't there."

Since I had the answer to my lead question, I saw no point in asking the second one about seeing or hearing something out of the ordinary. I also saw no point in sticking around Seville's version of Green Acres.

I thanked the quarrelsome handyman for his time and was about to leave when he said something that stopped me dead in my tracks.

"If you see that Salerno fella, tell him if he knows what's good for him, he'll stay the hell off my property."

"Salerno? Vincent Salerno? What are you talking about? I said, nearly knocking Mary into the wringer apparatus that dangled dangerously from the rusting remains of an old washing machine.

"That fella came snoopin' around there yesterday afternoon. Being that it was Sunday, I was out at the barn. At first, he said he was interested in buyin' a used ridin' mower. That's mostly what I do out there. I fix mowers and tractors."

Reaching into the back pocket of his greasy bib overalls, Abner Willson pulled out a small, dented flask. Removing the cork from it, he wiped the top the container with the sleeve of his dirty work shirt and took a long drink.

"What did he say or do that makes you think he was snooping around?" I asked. "It could be that he really was interested in purchasing the mower."

"Nah," the old man replied, "if that was the case, then how come he didn't buy it? You couldn't beat the price. I was practically givin' the damn thing away. Instead, he kept askin' me questions about Saturday mornin' around the time that the Deville woman was killed. I keep thinkin' about it. That man was up to somethin', you mark my words."

My feeling that the bodyguard and his alibi were key to the case returned stronger than before. I watched as Abner Wilson once again lifted the flask to his lips. But this time he didn't stop until the flask was empty. The liquor worked fast. Slurring his words, the handyman attempted to revisit the subject of a woman's place in society.

"Come on, Mar, I believe this is where we came in," I said, grabbing her with my one arm and waving good-bye to an oblivious Abner Wilson with the other. "If we hurry, there's one more stop I'd like to make before I call it a day."

"Oh, do you want me to take you to the hospital so you can visit with Charlie?" asked Mary as we climbed into her car. "That's no problem. In fact I was going to ask if you'd like to have dinner with me and Denny tonight. He's taking me to that new restaurant over in Springvale. Our reservation isn't until eight thirty, which gives you plenty of time to visit with Charlie before going to dinner with us."

"Thanks but no thanks. To begin with, the stop I was referring to is the Birdwells. You can just drop me off at Kettle Cottage. And in regard to your dinner invitation, if it's all the same to you, I'll take a rain check on it. Pesty's down in the dumps and I think she needs some TLC, so I'm having dinner with her. I thought I'd surprise her and have Milano's deliver her favorite meal — lasagna with meat sauce and extra cheese. Oh, and a pint of spumoni. She loves spumoni."

"What's with the stop at the Birdwells? Don't tell me you're going to confront Mr. Salerno. My stars, that could be dangerous. If he is the murderer, what's going to stop him from killing you? Maybe not right then and there, but later when you're not expecting it. You should wait until you hear from Horatio before doing anything like that. At least then you'll have a better idea of who and what you are dealing with, for heaven's sake. Use that brain of yours that Charlie is always bragging about."

And that's what I love about Mary. Just when I think she's a real bubblehead, she comes up with better advice than TV's Dr. Phil.

"Okay, you win. Home, James," I said as I lit a cigarette, opened the passenger window in the car and wondered if the little Kees would enjoy eating in the dining room for a change.

As things turned out, I didn't have to make that "one more stop" after all. Instead, the mountain (or in this instance, information concerning the mountain) came to me.

I'd almost finished clearing away the remains of the Milano's dinner when, to my surprise, Ellie Halsted called out my name as she knocked lightly on the back door of the kitchen.

"Come on in, it's open," I called out, forgetting that while it was true for the top half of the Dutch door, the same could not be said of the bottom half.

Because Ellie was a first-time visitor to Kettle Cottage, she found my invitation to be rather confusing. Tossing the empty spumoni container in the trash compactor, I hurried over to the door, unlatched the lower portion, and welcomed the girl into the kitchen.

My idea of treating Pesty's depression with two of the little Kees's favorite things, food and attention, worked. It was a truly pesty Pesty who greeted Ellie Halsted with a series of happy barks and the usual demand to be noticed and petted.

"Gosh, I love your kitchen and the colors you used — antique gold with touches of chocolate brown, crimson red, and apple green accents. I feel as though I've been transported to Tuscany. The walls look absolutely ancient, and I mean that in the nicest way," Ellie remarked.

"Why thank you," I said, pleased that nearly five years after the makeover, my kitchen still elicited positive comments from visitors.

I invited Ellie to sit down, which she did

on the padded window seat. "I've always dreamed of having a window seat like this but somehow it never worked out. Mother and I had very different ideas when it came to home decor. I've always favored American country while Mother preferred Scandinavian."

"Oh really? Is that what she had in mind for the old cottage?" I asked, curious to know if what I'd hoped to do with the place would have jelled with Dona's ideas.

"Yes," Ellie replied, "she wanted the entire interior paneled in white, bare wood floors, modern furniture, and no window treatments of any kind. She also wanted to put in a sauna, an exercise room, and of course, an outside deck complete with a huge hot tub. She said that she wanted the place to look as though it had been plucked from a rural town in Sweden."

"If you don't mind me saying, I think your mother missed the mark and confused Scandinavian practicality with modern minimalism, but that's neither here nor there. I'm sure that you didn't come here seeking decorating advice. So what's on your mind?"

Ellie sighed as she reached down and gently stroked Pesty's furry coat. "Oh, Mrs. Hastings, I hate to bother you and all, but

I've asked everyone else and you're the last person left. I hope you don't mind."

"Ask me what?" I said, stealing a quick look at the kitchen clock. I had to watch my time if I was going to visit Charlie. The hospital visiting hours were from one to three in the afternoon and from seven to nine in the evenings. So far my visiting record left a lot to be desired.

"When was the last time that you saw Vinny, you know, Mr. Salerno?" Ellie Halsted's face reflected the concern that I could hear in her voice.

"Let me think a minute. I guess it was yesterday at the Sunday breakfast buffet at the Birdwells. Why?"

"Because," said Ellie, shaking her head as if she herself could not believe what she was about to say, "he's missing."

CHAPTER TWENTY-TWO

Keeping my opinion and suspicions about Vincent Salerno to myself, and seeing how upset the girl was, I approached the subject with caution.

"Why don't you start at the beginning," I suggested, "and tell me about it. Maybe if you talk it out, we can shed some light on the situation."

"Remember when we were in Milano's yesterday in the late afternoon and you were asking me questions about Vinny?" said Ellie with a catch in her voice.

Since I wasn't sure where Ellie was going with her question, I tried to keep my answer as innocuous as possible. "Yes, I believe I asked if he'd been recently employed by your mother, or something like that."

"Yes, and I told you that my mother hired him after Auntie's death. Please, Mrs. Hastings, don't think I'm making much to do about nothing, which is what my father says, but right from the get-go, I suspected that there was more to it than my mother would admit."

"I'm sorry, Ellie, but I don't quite follow what you're saying. Can you run that by me again?"

I was dying for a cigarette but with my luck, the girl would turn out to be highly allergic to smoke and end up being rushed to the hospital. I reminded myself that if I didn't solve Dona Deville's murder soon, a certain young doctor wouldn't be available to marry Ellie, much less save her life. The cigarette would have to wait.

"What I'm saying, Mrs. Hastings, is that my mother was convinced Auntie's death wasn't an accident but happened because of my mother's drug abuse. Nobody, not even my father or Goody, paid attention to anything she had to say about it. Like everyone else who knew her, I thought she was losing it. And in a lot of ways, she was, but that doesn't make her death any easier to take. In spite of everything, I loved my mother and she loved me."

Eager to keep the conversation on track, I asked Ellie where Vincent Salerno fit into the picture. I didn't want to be too critical but I hinted strongly that in my opinion he didn't seemed to be much of a bodyguard.

Ellie's face brightened. "You know, Vinny told me that you were very perceptive. In fact, he said you'd make one heck of a private investigator because you have a sharp mind and a big nose. I hope that part about the nose doesn't offend you. That's just the way Vinny talks."

I could tell by the way the conversation was going, I probably would be late for my visit with Charlie.

"As you were saying, your mother thought her aunt's accident was no accident, so she bought a gun for protection and hired a bodyguard who was like a big brother and had bad work habits, like disappearing for hours, right? Maybe this time, the guy pulled a Judge Crater."

"Excuse me?" said the puzzled Ellie. "Who's Judge Crater?"

"A politically connected New York City judge who cleaned out his bank account, hopped in a taxi, and disappeared off the face of the earth. I believe it happened in the summer of 1930."

"Wow, that's like way, way, way before my time," said Ellie, scrutinizing every laugh line on my face.

"In case you're wondering, it's way, way before my time, too," I said, purposely using the word "way" only twice.

Ellie responded with her megawatt smile before returning to the subject of the missing bodyguard. "If he were going to be gone a really long time, he would have told me. The last person to see him was the bartender at Milano's. He said that Vinny was in the bar yesterday, late Sunday afternoon, when we were in the dining room. Vinny ordered a ginger ale, made a cell phone call, and the next thing the bartender knew, Vinny was gone. He didn't even finish his drink."

"It's only been about twenty-four hours since, as you say, he went missing," I said. "I really don't think that it's time to panic." Taking another peek at the clock on the wall, I resigned myself to the fact that unless Ellie wrapped things up pretty soon, my visit with Charlie would be a short one.

"I suppose you're right, but I keep thinking of something Vinny said to me about my mother's murder."

"And what was that?" I asked, hoping that what he'd said to Ellie made more sense than his alibi did for the time when Dona was murdered.

"He said that if my mother was right about Auntie's accident being no accident, then whoever murdered my mother probably murdered Auntie. And maybe they won't stop there."

Thanks to Hilly Murrow's reporting in print and on the air, everyone knew that Dona Deville's death made Ellie Halsted one very, very wealthy girl.

"Ellie, are you worried that you might be the murderer's next victim?"

"No, what I'm really worried about is that people might think I'm the one doing the killing," she answered. "Worse yet, they may even think that Peter is marrying me for my money."

I didn't see any value in bringing the obvious to Ellie's attention; she'd just provided herself and Peter Parker with one of the strongest motives for murder — monetary gain. After doing my best to assure Ellie that the missing Vinny would most likely turn up safe and sound, I walked her to the door, but not before promising her that I would attend her mother's funeral on Wednesday.

Then, without any time to review the conversation, freshen my makeup, or even change my clothes, I jumped in the van, lit a cigarette, and drove straight over to the hospital and my evening visit with Charlie.

I could have stayed at home for all the good it did me or my husband. Charlie was out like a light. The head nurse explained that during his physical therapy session with

Martha, he overdid it and was in pain. Dr. Parker ordered that Charlie be given something for the pain, which effectively knocked him out for the night. Since no one seemed the least bit concerned that my husband was dead to the world, I gave up and sat down in the bedside chair. Clutching Charlie's limp hand in mine, I dozed off. With our mouths shut, eyes closed, and intellects on hold, Charlie and I were alone together at long last.

We might have remained that way if it hadn't been for the panicky report made by a passerby claiming that he saw a couple of stiffs in room 321, Charlie's room. When my husband slept through the ensuing onslaught of invading hospital personnel, which included two janitors, a candy striper, a host of nurses, and the chaplain, I knew it was time for me to go home. And I did, but not before leaving my husband a note that read: *Here's looking at you, kid.* I didn't bother to sign it. He would know it was from me and that I'd been up to see him.

CHAPTER
TWENTY-THREE

Upon arriving home, I took a hot shower, poured myself a large glass of Weber's Bay Chardonnay, and collapsed with Pesty and the running shoe on the plaid camelback sofa in the dated but cozy den. I clicked on the TV in hopes of catching the last half hour of the *Antiques Roadshow* on PBS. I was in luck. I'd tuned in just as a retired schoolteacher was about to receive some exciting news from the appraiser. Much to the teacher's surprise, the grungy folk-art painting she'd inherited from an aunt was worth a pretty penny.

"See," I said to the little Kees, "you should never judge a book by its cover, especially one that's been inherited."

As soon as the words were out of my mouth, I all but fell off the sofa. Dona Deville had inherited something from an aunt — the old cottage. Had I overlooked the obvious? Was the cottage, like the folk-art painting, worth a pretty penny? Was the cottage part of the property dispute between Dona Deville and her ex-husband that Vincent Salerno alluded to when I asked him why Ruffy insisted on driving Ellie to Seville the night before Dona was murdered?

It was too late to contact Amanda Little, Seville's top real estate agent, regarding the property, but I added it to my Tuesday to-do list, along with stopping by Peter Parker's office. I wanted to hear his stethoscope explanation, that is, if he hadn't already been arrested for Dona's murder. But since Hilly Murrow hadn't trumpeted the news, nor had I heard anything from Martha Stevens or Ellie Halsted on the subject, I was pretty sure that for the time being, Peter Parker was still a free man.

"I feel like I'm missing something," I said to Pesty, who appeared to be more interested in her master's running shoe than in what I had to say. Later, when I climbed into bed, I found the shoe tucked under the pillow on my side of the four-poster brass bed. For her thoughtfulness, the little ball of fur was rewarded with an invitation to spend the night on Charlie's side of the bed, which she immediately accepted.

The next morning, Tuesday, I was awakened from a sound sleep by one hungry and pesty Kees. Scrambling into the only available clean outfit on my side of the bedroom closet, I vowed that if I accomplished nothing else, I would do a load of wash before the sun set. Maybe I was getting used to the thing but after checking myself out in the full-length mirror in the downstairs hallway, I thought I looked pretty good in the green chenille jumpsuit.

"Ho, ho, ho," I said when JR answered the phone. "Guess who's calling."

"Don't tell me, I think I know. Since you sound too long in the tooth to be Little Sprout, you must be the Jolly Green Giant. What's on that fertile, or should I say furtive, mind of yours this morning, Mother? And make it quick. Matt's in the bedroom getting ready to leave and I'm supposed to be fixing him breakfast."

"Are you telling me that you can't cook and talk at the same time? Where did I fail?" I shot back as I overfilled the coffeemaker, flooding the countertop with water.

"Come on, Mother, get to the point, I really don't have much time," said JR.

"Okay, I just thought I'd give you a call so that you know what I'm up to today. I'll be going over to see Peter Parker at his office. Actually it's Doc's office, but you know

181

what I mean. And before you ask, there's nothing wrong with me. I want to ask him about the stethoscope."

"Do me a favor, promise me you won't go there alone. Either get Aunt Mary to go with you or wait for me. Kelly's got baseball practice at ten and it's my turn to drive. Oh, and I have to bring the cat to the vet clinic for some kind of shots. Get a load of this — they think she's allergic to fish."

"Don't forget about me, Mama," cried a small but insistent voice that I correctly guessed was Kerry's. "You promised to take me to the Springvale mall for my ballet outfit. I'm the only girl in the class who doesn't have a tutu."

"Listen, Kerry," I overheard JR speaking to my granddaughter despite an attempt to muffle the conversation, "Grandma needs me to run an errand with her today, so maybe we'll go to the mall tomorrow."

"But that's what you said yesterday," wailed Kerry. "My lesson is tomorrow and Mrs. Duckworth expects me to have a tutu. I've got to have a tutu."

"What the heck is a tutu?" asked Matt in a voice loud enough to wake the dead. I could have used him the night before when I was visiting Charlie at the hospital.

"Hey, JR," I hollered into the phone, "I'll

let you go and I promise I'll take Aunt Mary with me. Love ya."

"Love ya, too, Mom. Maybe next time. And like I said before, if I think of anything that might be of some help, I promise I'll call you on your cell no matter what, when, or where."

There are times when I miss not having kids around but this was not one of those days. I doubted if JR remembered the trip I'd made years ago to Indianapolis in the middle of a severe thunderstorm warning. Like Matt, Charlie also demanded to know "what the heck is a tutu?"

Whatever it was that I did to the coffee-maker, the thing wasn't working. I put the kettle on, deciding instant coffee would have to do, dropped two pieces of sourdough bread into the toaster, and dumped a measured cup of Dandy Diet dog food into Pesty's food dish.

Once breakfast was out of the way, I put in a call to Mary. After listening to my plans for the day, she enthusiastically volunteered to tag along.

"Denny's taking a day off from golf to work down at the store," Mary said. "That surpised me almost as much as Herbie showing up today. In view of what happened to him last night, I felt sure that he would ask for the day off."

"What's his problem? Did the little green men keep Herbie up past his bedtime again?" My inquiry was loaded with much sarcasm and little sympathy.

The furniture store salesman's claims of being abducted by aliens and transported to their spaceships, where he's prodded and probed, had become old hat. If Herbie is to be believed, he's logged more time in outer space than the Russian cosmonauts who manned the Mir station.

"No, not at all," replied Mary, deliberately ignoring my snide reference to Herbie's nocturnal activities. "His car was broken into last night along with three other cars on Sixth Street. He's really upset about the whole thing. Not only did the thieves take almost everything that wasn't nailed down in the car, they also made off with his brand-new bowling shirt. It had his name on it and everything."

"Jeez, that really is too bad. You know, when you think about it, Seville has had more than its fair share of this kind of thing. Most of it seems to be happening in and around the college and the downtown area."

"You're right about that, Gin. Are you going to mention it to Matt?"

"No, I don't think so. I have a feeling that

Matt is very much aware of the situation. As my mother was fond of saying, unless you're the boss, don't tell the workers how to do their jobs."

"Really? Funny, I don't remember your mother ever saying anything like that," Mary said, sounding skeptical.

"Well, she did," I fibbed, anxious to move on. I advised Mary to wear something cool and comfortable in keeping with the weather forecast of another hot and humid day. "I'll pick you up in about fifteen minutes. Bye-bye."

Before leaving Kettle Cottage, I made sure that the air conditioner was set low enough to suit Pesty. I also filled her bowl with cold water and a handful of ice cubes. When the pampered pooch spotted the keys to the van in my hand, she dashed to the back door. Charlie's running shoe dangled from her mouth by a soggy shoestring.

"Sorry, girl, I can't take you with today. It's too hot," I said to the disappointed pooch, who began to whine in protest.

Taking the shoe from Pesty, I filled it up with a selection of diet dog biscuits. With the pampered pooch close on my heels, I set the shoe down under the kitchen table. The combination of shoe and biscuits did the trick. When I reminded Pesty to behave

185

and that I would be back soon, she was up to her short snoot in treats. Thus occupied, the little Kees ignored my departure.

On the drive to Mary's, I thought about the rash of car break-ins and the growing number of home burglaries. So far, no one had gotten hurt since none of the home owners were present when the thieves hit. I also thought about Dona Deville's murder and the death of her aunt. Were all these events somehow connected? I honestly didn't know, but my mind kept replaying the old nursery rhyme that began "This is the house that Jack built . . ."

The simple but clever rhyme begins with that one line and ends with it as well, forming a circle. Was it possible that, like the nursery rhyme, my investigation would end up in a circle? I could only hope that the circle wouldn't form a noose around some innocent person's neck. Where, I wondered, was my Irish intuition when I needed it?

CHAPTER TWENTY-FOUR

"Yes, Chief Stevens told me my stethoscope was found at the murder scene and Dr. Loo indentified it as being the murder weapon. I'll tell you the same thing I told the chief. I didn't even know the darn thing was missing. I thought I'd mislaid it and without giving it a second thought, I used my uncle's spare," said Peter Parker, gesturing at the mountain of assorted junk, which included boxes of old files, charts, and outdated medical paraphernalia. The stuff looked as though it was ready to take over any available space, starting with Peter's desk. Think *Little Shop of Horrors* with a medical twist.

"My stars," Mary exclaimed to Peter, "how on earth can you find anything in this . . ."

"I believe the word you're searching for is *mess,* or maybe *disaster,*" said Helen McCordle, Doc Parker's longtime nurse and receptionist, as she stood in the middle of the tiny office with her hands on her hips.

Everything about the fiftysomething woman, from the top of her nurse's cap down to the tip of her white shoes, was as neat as a pin. Even her hazel eyes matched her blond, brown, and gray hair. She was neither short nor tall and I didn't detect any unnecessary poundage on her trim body. I also felt for sure that Helen McCordle's underwear was neat, starched, and ironed. Why in the world, I thought to myself, with someone like Helen at the helm, was Peter's office in such disarray? I was about to find out.

"I told him to use Doc's office, you know, the one he sees his patients in and keeps all nice and tidy," said Helen. "But did he listen? Oh no. Instead, Dr. Peter plunks himself down in this closet. Doc only uses the area for storage and the occasional poker session with the boys. The room hasn't had a proper cleaning in maybe ten or even twenty years. Personally, I don't think it's very healthy in here," sniffed Helen. "But then I'm only the nurse, not the doctor."

With her aquiline nose pointed toward the ceiling in a show of disapproval, Helen McCordle returned to her own domain, the neat-as-a-pin cubicle that was separated from the waiting area by a sparkling-clean sliding-glass partition.

Apparently feeling the need to explain why he chose the storage-cum-poker-room over Doc's tidy and organized office, Peter launched into what sounded to me like a well-rehearsed speech.

"I thought if I could show my uncle how well two doctors could function in relatively close quarters while still maintaining the needed privacy, then perhaps he wouldn't mind my being around on a permanent basis. It's something that would be beneficial to both our lives. Now all I have to do is to get the place cleaned out and shipshape before Aunt Lucy and Uncle Doc return from Hawaii. Come back in a week or so and I guarantee you won't recognize the place."

Thanking the young doctor for his time and his explanation regarding the stethoscope, I signaled to Mary that it was time for us to leave. We stepped out of the small, air-conditioned medical building and into the heat. We were almost to where I'd parked the van when I thought of something I'd forgotten to check out with the nurse/receptionist. Since neither Peter nor Helen had reported a break-in at the medical center, I wondered if someone might have swiped the stethoscope on Friday during office hours. With Helen McCordle manning the reception desk, more than likely she would have insisted that everyone wanting to see the doctor put their signature on the sign-in sheet. Maybe I could find a name that had a connection to my investigation. As Mary continued walking to the van, I sprinted back to the medical building and Helen's neat-as-a-pin cubicle.

"He's on the phone," said Helen barely glancing up from the stack of paperwork on her desk. "Can I help you?"

"I sure hope so," I said, "but I can see that this isn't the best time to bother you." Maybe my mother didn't say it, but I knew all about catching flies with honey.

"Hey, I'm always busy, but that doesn't mean that I can't take time out to help someone. Now what can I do for you?" Less than five minutes later, I returned to the van with a copy of Friday's sign-in sheet tucked in my purse.

Ten minutes later, Mary and I were sitting in Amanda Little's chichi family room/real estate office. "I'll be with you ladies in a minute," Amanda crooned, placing her manicured fingers over the mouthpiece of the white and gold French-style telephone. Everything, from the carpeting on the floor to the cove ceiling, was gold and white, including Amanda Little.

Dressed from head to toe in a white sundress with gold trim, white shoes, and gold jewelry, and with her white, flawless skin and shining gold hair, Amanda Little looked absolutely beautiful. The darling of our town's chamber of commerce, the highly repected Realtor had, not once but three times, been named Seville's Business Person of the Year.

"If there's such a thing as reincarnation," Mary whispered to me, "I want to come back as her."

"Really? Not me," I whispered to Mary, "I want to come back as her interior designer. Whoever it was must have laughed all the way to the bank. Throw in a couple of gold-painted cupids and some rose petals and you've got yourself a Vegas wedding chapel."

In less time than it took to convince the dynamic Amanda Little that I wasn't interested in buying, selling, leasing, flipping, trading, or any other options she claimed were tailor-made for people in my age group, I learned that no one, not even squatters, were interested in the old cottage or in the land itself. I had come to another dead end. Or so I thought, until Amanda revealed the latest gossip that was making the rounds in the real estate world. I believe the aggressive Amanda mentioned it on the chance that I might have picked up some additional information from the Deville people. She let it be known that the Hershfield Corporation, one of the largest hotel chains in the Midwest, was interested in acquiring Dona's Den. The health spa was situated on what Amanda described as a hot piece of prime real estate in the heart of downtown Indy.

"With Indianapolis pushing to become the place for conventions, all the major hotel chains, especially Hershfield, are anxious to get in on the action," said Amanda, tossing her mane of golden hair over her shoulder.

Lowering her voice as if the walls had ears, she hinted that even a certain New York multimillionaire known for his marriages and distinctive hairstyle had already approached Ruffy Halsted with a really sweet offer.

"Ruffy Halsted? Why him and not Dona?" I wanted to know.

"Apparently, he was tired of dealing with Dona. Since the property was jointly owned by Dona and her ex, he felt once he got Ruffy on his side, then it would be easier to convince Dona that it was time to sell. You throw Hershfield into the mix and it stands to reason that somebody is going to make megabucks on the deal," Amanda informed me, twirling a lock of her golden hair.

I could tell from the tone of her voice, along with the look she gave me, the woman was having second thoughts about my ability to grasp the importance of what she'd just revealed. I really didn't care what she thought, I was just pleased that I now had a pretty good idea what Ruffy discussed with Ellie on their ride down to Seville Friday night.

The ringing of Amanda Little's phone brought our visit with her to an end, which was fine with me. The overabundance of white and gold on the walls, floor, furniture, and on Amanda Little herself was starting make my head ache.

There was one thing left on my Tuesday to-do list and it involved Horatio. I wanted to find out if he'd come up with anything on the bodyguard, Vincent Salerno. Rather than risk another run-in with the "happy housekeeper," Mrs. Daggert, I decided to call Horatio on his cell phone. I also decided that the call could wait until after lunch and my afternoon visit with Charlie.

While other cities and towns experience traffic congestion in the early morning and late afternoon, Seville's traffic congestion occurs at lunchtime.

Lunchtime in Seville can start as early as eleven a.m. or as late as one p.m., but it can't be missed. In our town, a person can be forgiven for a virtual laundry list of things but failing to show up for lunch, be it served at home or on the job, in a small cafe or at a fancy restaurant, is tantamount to stomping on the flag. In other words, it just isn't done, at least not in the heart of popcorn country. As a result of the residents of Seville's devotion to their midday meal, driving through the town at lunchtime can be as challenging as traversing Germany's autobahn in a homemade go-cart.

Seeking to avoid the traffic buildup on Main Street, I made a quick left-hand turn into a small half street and then a right-hand turn onto Lincoln Avenue. If I had all the twists and turns straight in my head, and I believed that I did, a short trip down the alley behind England's Fine Furniture, followed by a right-hand turn onto Washington, and I would be only a half block away from the Koffee Kabin with its adjoining parking lot.

With my right-hand turn signal blinking, I was about to make the turn onto Washington when Mary let out a loud whoop followed by her command that I stop the van, which I did.

"Jeez, Mary, what on earth are you yelling about?" I asked in about as pleasant of a voice as you can imagine under the circumstances.

"Really, Jean," huffed Mary. "I was merely trying to save you from having a head-on collision. You were about to enter the wrong way on a one-way street."

"One-way? Since when?" I asked. "Where's the sign?"

"Since yesterday," said Mary, readjusting the slack in her seat belt, "and the new sign is being put up today. According to what I read in this morning's newspaper, the juvenile who painted the word *no* over the word *one* on the original sign has already fessed up to the prank and will have to pay for the new sign."

Clicking off the turn signal, I drove around the block and ended up parking the van in the same space I'd parked it when Mary and I visited Peter Parker earlier that morning. My driving, like my investigation, seemed to be going in a circle.

CHAPTER
TWENTY-FIVE

"Hello, Horatio? What? Wait, I'm having a hard time understanding you. No, there's nothing wrong with my hearing. Let me walk out on the patio. Sometimes the reception is better out there. What? No, I didn't say anything about a wedding reception. I said . . . Hello, hello."

Sitting on the back steps of Kettle Cottage and glaring at the cell phone in my hand, I wasn't sure if I'd lost the call or the call had lost me. After three attempts to reconnect with my friend Horatio Bordeaux, I gave up and returned to the kitchen and deposited the cell phone in my purse.

"There's something to be said for the old days when Ma Bell was in charge," I said to Pesty, who was busy ridding the kitchen floor of crumbs. "Back then, a dropped call only occurred when your mother or father got on the extension and told you in no uncertain terms to get off the phone."

The little Kees wasn't particulary interested in what I had to say since nothing I'd said contained any of her favorite words such as cheese, cookies, curly fries, or taco chips.

Venturing out from under the kitchen table, Pesty made the short trip over to her bowl, where she used the tip of her pink tongue to test the temperature of the water. Finding that the ice cubes had melted, she turned away in disgust, picked up the running shoe and deposited it, along with her pudgy self, at my feet.

"I hate to bother you with my problems, my furry friend, but right now you're the only one available to listen to my woes. Take this afternoon for instance. I went over to the hospital to visit Charlie only to find his bed empty. I was told it was his bath time. As usual, no one knew when he left or when he'd be back. I waited over half an hour before giving up. I left him another note. This one said: *Roses are red, violets are blue. I hope you miss me as much as I miss you.* I signed your name. Pretty clever, right?"

Pesty responded with a yawn. Some dog experts claim that's a sign of anxiety. This Kees wasn't anxious; she was bored.

Leaving the pampered pooch to work it

out, I let my fingers do the walking through the yellow pages, got the number I needed, and using the kitchen phone, called Twall and Sons Mortuary.

Mr. Twall Sr. informed me that the service for Dona Deville would be held the next day, Wednesday, in the Morning Glory Room at eleven fifteen a.m., and it would be followed by a catered luncheon at Birdwell's Bed and Breakfast on Blueberry Lane.

"Shall I tell the family that you will be joining them?" inquired the senior Mr. Twall in his soft, dry-as-dust voice. "Or would you prefer it be a surprise?"

I was tempted to tell him that when it comes to wakes and funerals, especially my own, I would prefer to be a no-show. Suspecting the elderly undertaker wouldn't see the humor in my personal preference, I politely informed him that I'd been invited by a close family member.

The next person I called was Mary, who agreed to accompany me to Wednesday's service and luncheon. I followed my call to Mary with one to JR.

"Sorry, Mom, no can do. With Matt spending practically every waking minute on an investigation I'm not at liberty to discuss, I've been doing double duty around here. Tomorrow is going to be another supermom day, if you know what I mean," said JR, sounding tired and tearful.

I was immediately overcome with guilt. I didn't need my Irish intuition to tell me that my pregnant daughter was in need of some TLC and that I needed to get my priorities straight.

"I understand completely, JR. Now that that's out of the way maybe we can talk about the main reason for my call," I said, thinking fast.

"Oh? Is something wrong?" JR asked.

"Only if you and the twins turn down an invitation to have dinner with me and a certain Kentucky colonel tonight. I've got peppermint ice cream and butter cookies for dessert."

"Name the time and we'll be there," said JR, sounding better already.

"Give me time to phone in my order and a little extra to run out and pick up the ice cream and cookies. How about I see you here in thirty minutes or so?"

"It all works for me, Mom, especially the dessert, but if you already have it, how come you have to stop at the store to pick it up?"

"Because, Missy Smartypants, I fibbed about the dessert. See you and the twins in a little bit."

"Right, and Mom," JR said, catching me

just as I was about to say good-bye, "thanks."

"Don't thank me, thank the colonel, Ben and Jerry, and Nabisco," I answered, gathering up my purse and keys in preparation for my chicken, ice cream, and cookie run.

"Mother," said JR, sounding more like her old, spunky self, "I'm not thanking you for that. I'm thanking you for being my mom. Love ya. Bye-bye."

Tuesday night's dinner with the colonel, JR, and the twins was a great success. While Kerry and Kelly watched TV in the den, JR and I spent some quality time together. I listened while she talked about everything from national politics to the lack of fashionable maternity clothes and everything in between. JR's problem wasn't that she needed a shoulder to cry on but rather she needed to share her thoughts with another grown-up. Explaining that to a man is like trying to explain Einstein's theory of relativity to the Three Stooges.

It was close to eight p.m. when a talked-out JR and a restless set of twins kissed me good night and returned to their house on Tall Timber Road. If I hurried, I'd be able to get to the hospital before evening visiting hours were over.

Not bothering to stop at the desk in the

lobby for a visitor's pass, I pressed the button for the elevator and was instantly rewarded with an empty car and a quick ride to the third floor. Dropping off a box of assorted chocolate creams, along with a note of thanks to the hospital staff, at the seemingly deserted nurses station, I made the now-familiar trip down the hall to Charlie's room.

The door to his room was closed, which is generally not a good sign in a hospital setting. As I stood there weighing the pros and cons of pushing the door open, I was startled by the head nurse who seemed to appear out of nowhere.

"Mrs. Hasting, how did you get up here?" she demanded. "The volunteer at the desk in the lobby was given strict orders not to issue any visitor passes for room 321."

"Why on earth not?" I asked. Then I had a thought so terrible the words seemed to stick so tight in my throat and it actually hurt when I finally got them out. "Oh, dear God . . . Charlie . . . is he . . . is he . . ."

"Dead?" the nurse finished for me. "No, he's fine except he has a rash all over his chest, neck, and arms. Dr. Parker was in to see him at suppertime and ordered some tests to be run. Until we know what we're dealing with, your husband's been quarantined," she said, lifting my hand from the middle of the door so that I could see and read the posted notice.

I left another note for Charlie. The head nurse, obviously a World War II buff as is my husband, smiled as she read the one word message: *Nuts!* If Brigadier General McAuliffe thought it an appropriate response to the German demand that he surrender at Bastogne rather than fight on, then it was good enough for Charlie. I didn't bother to sign the note.

I was walking toward where I'd parked the van in the hospital's brightly lit parking lot when I heard someone call my name. Turning around, I spotted Horatio Bordeaux sitting behind the wheel of a new, fire-engine-red van that had been modified to fit his special needs.

"Pretty neat, huh," said the well-educated, well-mannered Horatio, sounding like a young boy with his first two-wheel bicycle.

"Why, I think it's even better than neat. Dude, you got yourself some real cool wheels. When did you get it?"

"I was over at Stanford Motors picking it up when you called me. Incidentally, I want to apologize for our abbreviated conversation. I think it was my fault. I was in Cord Stanford's office signing papers and writing checks and all that kind of stuff. I guess I was rather excited and was all thumbs. I tried to call you back but somehow managed to goof that up as well."

"Horatio, stop with the apology. I'm the one who should be saying I'm sorry. You told me that as soon as you had something for me on Vincent Salerno you'd let me know. But you know me, I want to know everything, even before it happens. By the way, what are you doing here? You're not ill, are you?"

The thought that Horatio, a diabetic, might be in for another bad time with his health made my heart hurt. After Mary, he is probably my closest friend. I was relieved when he explained that he'd stopped at the hospital to drop off some reports he'd been working on for the hospital's office of security.

"I was about to head over to your place when I noticed you walking across the lot," he said as he reached across the seat and snapped open his briefcase, removed a large, unmarked envelope, and handed it to me.

I didn't have to ask what was in the envelope. I knew it was the report on Vincent Salerno.

"Oh, Horatio, you're something else. Have

you got time for a cup of coffee? I'm buying. Or if you prefer, we can have tea at Kettle Cottage."

"Any other time I'd say yes, but with the tornado warnings and all, I think I better get home. You, too, Jeannie. From the looks of that sky, we're in for some really nasty weather."

CHAPTER
TWENTY-SIX

As usual, Horatio was right. The storm hit about ten minutes after I had arrived at Kettle Cottage. In central Indiana, a tornado warning is synonymous with the loss of cable TV, which happened just as the weather bureau was announcing the names of the towns that were in the direct path of the approaching storm.

Normally, I would've called it a night, hopped into bed, and with Pesty clinging to me like a strip of double-sided tape, been fast asleep, leaving Charlie to deal with the storm and its aftermath. Years ago, we agreed that certain jobs were better handled by the wife and others by the husband. Thanks to gender equality, my workload continues to decrease while Charlie's continues to increase. But Charlie wasn't home, so it became my job to hold down the fort, or in this case, the house.

Running to the bay window in the kitchen

to see if it was time for Pesty and me to seek shelter in the lowest level of our home, I heard a tremendous crack of lightning as Kettle Cottage was plunged into darkness. There is nothing like a tornado warning that comes in the night to renew one's faith in a Supreme Being or whatever name we mortals give the powers that be.

Thanks to the workers at the Seville Power and Light Co-op, the electricity was restored after a short time and I was able to return to Horatio's report, my investigation notes, and the copy of Peter Parker's patient check-in sheet for the Friday before Dona Deville's murder.

Horatio's report disclosed that Vincent Albert Salerno was a native of Chicago, a graduate of DePaul University, decorated veteran of Vietnam, and a divorced father of three. After spending almost seven years with the FBI as a special investigator, Vincent Salerno took early retirement and became a licensed private investigator specializing in examining unusual auto fatalities. Hired by the company that had insured Dona Deville's late aunt, Vincent Salerno was assigned to look into the old lady's death. Since everyone around Dona knew she was paranoid about her daughter's safety, he and Dona agreed that the job as

Ellie's bodyguard would be the perfect cover for the investigator. The company had not heard from Vincent since he called on his cell phone Sunday afternoon. They agreed to notify Horatio should any new info regarding the case and/or Salerno surface. End of report. I fervently hoped that it wasn't the end of the missing investigator.

By the time I was ready to call it a night, I had my own theory about who had murdered the diet diva. I found myself in agreement with Vincent Salerno's hypothesis that whoever was responsible for Dona's death was probably also responsible for the elderly aunt's death. The motive though, like Salerno's puzzling alibi about looking for signs of change, continued to be a mystery to me.

On an impulse, instead of gathering up the patient check-in list, my notes, the report, and stacking everything in a neat pile, I spread the paperwork in a circle, along the edge of the round oak table. As I did so, the nursery rhyme about the house that Jack built repeated itself in my head.

Staring at the papers on the tabletop, it dawned on me that just as the rhyme started with the name of Jack, my circle started with the name of the person I believed was the murderer, thanks to Helen McCordle's neat-as-a-pin patient check-in sheet.

Because my investigation wasn't quite complete, I left a space in the circle. But if my hunch was right, then soon, very soon, both the case and the circle would be closed.

CHAPTER TWENTY-SEVEN

"Why aren't you wearing black?" Mary asked as she opened the passenger door of the van and eased herself into the seat. "We are going to Dona's funeral, aren't we?"

"Yes, we are," I said, answering Mary's last question before tackling the first, which needed a longer and more carefully worded answer. I certainly didn't want to upset Mary or even hint that she might be out of step with the current dos and don'ts of today's fashion police.

Mary and I belong to the generation that grew up always adhering to certain rules of fashion, such as never wear white before Memorial Day or after Labor Day; bikini swimsuits, short shorts, and miniskirts shouldn't be worn by any woman over the age of thirty; only the bride wears white to the wedding; and black attire is a must when attending a wake or a funeral. Naturally, the always accomodating Mary was dressed from head to toe in black.

"This outfit was my only choice," I said, as we began the short drive from Mary's house to Twall and Sons Mortuary on Washington Street. "Everything else was in the washer when last night's storm hit and knocked out the electricity. I really don't think Dona Deville will care what I'm wearing and the rest of the people probably won't notice."

"My stars, I think a teal top and a white, flouncy skirt will be noticed. Please tell me that the skirt is lined."

"No, it's not, but before you have an apoplexy, I am wearing a half-slip and if you notice, my purse is black."

For Mary, the fact that my white sandal shoes didn't match my purse was too much. "Listen, Gin, if you walk in lugging that monstrosity you call a purse, I'm walking out."

"Speaking of purses, where's yours, Mar? If you left it at home, it's going to have to stay there. It's already eleven and you know what a stickler the senior Mr. Twall is about starting on time."

"Well then, I guess it's going to have to stay there. Maybe you can swing by the house on our way over to the luncheon at the Birdwells'. I hope Sally's having Billy do the catering. His tiny little sandwiches are to die for."

Mary was in the middle of carrying on about Billy's culinary skills when I turned the van into the mortuary's parking lot.

"Jeez, all the spots are filled. I'm going to have to cut down the alley and take a chance on finding a parking place on Washington. Why don't you get out here and go in without me. I'll catch up," I suggested to Mary, thinking that I was doing her a favor.

"Not on your life, Gin. You know how I feel about seeing dead people. Look what happened the last time I saw Dona."

In retrospect, I was glad that Mary stuck with me as I circled the block in search of an empty parking space. If she hadn't done so, the solution to the missing Vincent Salerno's puzzling alibi might have remained a mystery.

"Now don't forget, Washington is a one-way street," Mary said in a tone of voice that really irritated me.

"I couldn't even if I wanted to, thanks to you," I replied through clenched teeth. "You screamed so loudly yesterday you practically broke my eardrums."

"And what was I supposed to do, Jean? Just sit there and say nothing while you crashed into oncoming traffic like Dona's aunt did? What kind of person would do that? I'm surprised you haven't blamed me for the missing sign." Mary wasn't surprised but she was angry.

Neither one of us had much to say after that and things pretty much stayed that way as we walked the short distance from where I'd finally parked the van to the mortuary.

"Mary, wait a minute," I said, stopping under Twall's trademark purple-and-black canopy. "I'm sorry, I didn't mean to be so snippy. Forgive me?"

"Sure, I do. And I'm sorry if I irritated you, Gin. I was only trying to be helpful. Like I said, what kind of a person would I be if I didn't do anything."

"Right, and you're right about the possible dire consequences had you not screamed," I reminded Mary before following up with the familiar one word that always ends our petty misunderstandings. "Friends?"

"You betcha. Friends," Mary replied, and in an attempt to put a different spin on the incident, she added, "You know, Gin, when you think about it, the one to blame is the kid who changed the original sign to read NO WAY."

"You got that right," I answered as I locked arms with Mary and walked into

Twall and Sons Mortuary where, according to the advertisement on the billboard that can be seen from the interstate: TWALL AND SONS TREATS EVERY BODY LIKE ROYALTY!

Unaware that the cars in the mortuary's parking lot, for the most part, belonged to people attending the Claude Hawkins funeral service being held in the Rose Room, I was shocked and surprised to see how few people had come to Dona Deville's funeral service. Had it not been for a small contingent of townies, most of whom were business aquaintences rather than friends of the deceased, the entourage, minus the missing bodyguard, and the senior Mr. Twall would have been the only people in attendance.

When the elderly Mr. Twall stepped to the podium to begin the eulogy, Ellie Halsted, flanked by Ruffy Halsted and Dr. Peter Parker, sat down in the first row of chairs.

Marsha Gooding (Goody), Todd Masters, Maxine Roberts, and Hilly Murrow were seated in the row directly behind the trio. Todd and Maxine held hands (a pretty good indication that the two had "kissed and made up") while Goody stared stonily ahead. Hilly Murrow balanced a notepad on her bony, crossed legs. With pen in hand, she struck a pose reminiscent of Rosalind

Russell's screen portrayal of a smart, sexy, tough-talking newspaper reporter. If not for the ban on smoking, a smoldering cigarillo would have been clamped between our star reporter's oversize choppers.

The next row was taken up by Sally Bird-well, Abner Wilson, Herbie Waddlemeyer, Rollie Stevens, and Dona's thought-to-be-long-lost first love, Kurt Summerfield. Despite the passage of time, he was recognized by all of us townies. The years had been very kind to him. He was as handsome as ever.

"Oh my stars, if I'm not mistaken, that's Kurt Summerfield," Mary exclaimed in an Irish whisper. Her voice bounced over the empty row of chairs that separated us from the others. With Mary by my side, I had a wide-angle view of everyone in attendance, including the person whom I believed was responsible for two and possibly three murders.

Anxious to keep a low profile, I used my own version of sign language to convey a message to Mary that she should cool it for the time being. She answered with an affirmative wink.

In his dry-as-dust voice, the mortician droned on for nearly an hour, crediting Dona Deville with every virtue known to humankind and then some. I suspected the eulogy was crafted by Maxine Roberts in an attempt to reap some positive press, via Hilly Murrow, out of a negative situation, something that surely would be a plus on Maxine's résumé.

Dona's body had been cremated, which eliminated the viewing of the body and the usual scramble by family and friends to come up with loving, memorable remarks about the deceased. In Dona's case, judging from everything that I'd learned about the diet diva, it would have been a real challenge. Although I must admit that I would've loved to have had the opportunity to observe the murderer in that type of situation. Dona's cremation made things easier for everyone, including her killer.

I was beginning to doubt that the eulogy was ever going to end when the senior Mr. Twall began what amounted to a litany of thanks. I think the thing we were all most thankful for was that the ordeal was almost over. By the time the poor man got around to thanking us for joining in "this celebration of the life of a woman who had given so much of herself to others," everyone, including yours truly, was ready and eager to move on to the final phase of Dona's send-off: catered lunch at

Sally Birdwell's house.

Seeing that the luncheon was in close proximity to Kettle Cottage, I parked the van in my own driveway and took a minute to run in and check on Pesty before going to Sally's.

My purse was still in the back of the van. Knowing that smoking was allowed on the redwood deck, I fished the cigarette case and cell phone from the bottom of my purse before returning it to the van. Tucking the case into the single pocket of my skirt, I was about to do the same with the cell phone, but Mary, who was standing on the drive waiting for me, offered to put the phone in her skirt pocket. Because the luncheon wasn't exactly a festive occasion, I set the phone on vibrate so as not to disturb anyone with the cancan music I'd chosen as an alternative to the standard telephone ring.

CHAPTER TWENTY-EIGHT

We were welcomed to the luncheon by Ellie, who, like everyone else, was dry-eyed and in pretty good spirits considering the solemn nature of the occassion. Standing next to her was Kurt Summerfield.

"I believe you two already know Mr. Summerfield," said Ellie. "Wasn't it nice of him to drive in from Indianapolis for the service? Mother would have been so pleased."

"And surprised," Mary added, beaming at the former basketball star and prom king of Seville High. "How long have you lived in Indy?"

"I moved there about two weeks after graduation. I had a chance to go into business with a relative and took him up on it," Kurt answered, matching Mary beam for beam, "and as things turned out, it was a damn good chance. Five years ago, I bought out the relative and I'm happy to say that now I'm the sole owner of Fantastic Towels."

"Well, good for you," said Mary, "I'm not familiar with that brand but next time I buy paper towels, I'll look for yours."

"Mr. Summerfield's company doesn't manufacture paper towels or any other kind of towel. Fantastic is a towel service company that provides towels and linens for almost every private health club in the Indy area," Marsha Gooding said, elbowing Mary out of the way.

To me, it was obvious from the looks Goody and Kurt exchanged that they had more than a nodding acquaintance.

"And was Dona's Den one of those?" I asked, directing my question to Kurt Summerfield. Again it was the personal assistant who provided the answer.

"Let's just say we were about to enter into negotiations but then Dona gets herself murdered and we're back to where we started."

Goody didn't clarify her use of the personal pronoun "we," leaving me to wonder about her allegiance. I had serious doubts that Dona would've been all that pleased or even surprised with Kurt Summerfield's appearance at her funeral service.

"Afternoon, Miz Hastings, Miz England," Abner Wilson said as Mary and I moved from the foyer into the dining room.

Attired in a pair of new overalls, white dress shirt, and tie, the old man looked clean and sober. "I want to thank you," he said as he filled his plate with a selection of finger foods from the scrumptious buffet courtesy of Billy Birdwell's fledgling catering service.

Abner Wilson's thanks took me by surprise. "You're welcome," I replied, "but what are you thanking me for?"

"For takin' care of that Salerno fella. I ain't seen hide nor hair of him since I told you to tell him to stay away from my barn property."

"If that's the case, then thank yourself, not me. Like everyone else, I haven't seen or heard from him since Sunday."

"Some of them college boys that help me out think he's the one who broke into those cars Monday night," said the old man in a stage whisper.

I was saved from any further conversation about the missing bodyguard by, of all people, Herbie Waddlemeyer. The man may have a pumpkin head but he's got the ears of a fox. Upon hearing Abner Wilson's comment about the car break-ins, Herbie the victim was eager and ready to talk to anyone who would listen about the tragic loss of his bowling shirt, the one with his name on it.

I made my excuses to both Abner and Herbie and ducked out to the redwood deck. Taking the case from my pocket, I lit a cigarette and thought about what I hoped would be the next and final step in my investigation. It was Mary's earlier comment about the real culprit being the person who'd changed the sign on Washington Street that pointed my mind in the right direction. Or perhaps it was Dona herself who reached back from the great beyond to assist me in the investigation. Either way, Vincent Salerno's alibi, a puzzle within a puzzle, finally made sense.

I recalled the Sunday morning when Salerno told me, "My horoscope said that I should watch for signs of change, so Saturday morning I got in my car and went looking for them." And I thought about Horatio's report on Salerno — he was really investigating the death of Dona Deville's aunt who, for no apparent reason, headed the wrong way down the highway. And I thought about how signs can be intentionally changed . . .

"Mind if I join you?" Not waiting for my answer, Ruffy Halsted stepped out on the redwood deck and planted himself about two feet away from where I was standing.

"I didn't realize that you're a smoker," I

said as I instinctively stepped back.

"I ain't," he replied, "but I used to be. I still miss it, even the smell. You know you really should give up. It ain't healthy. It's almost as bad as all them drugs Dona got hooked on. Ironic, ain't it?"

Not sure what he meant, I asked a question of my own. "Is that a comment on how your former wife lived or on how she died?"

"You know somethin', lady, the police chief just got done tellin' me about how you fancy yourself to be a detective. He warned me about talkin' to you."

"The name is Jean Hastings, and that's Mrs. Hastings to you, chum. Now, if you'll excuse me, I'm going back into the dining room. Here," I said, handing him what was left of my cigarette, "since you miss smoking so much you can have it. I'm finished with it, you, and our conversation."

Leaving the openmouthed Ruffy Halsted in my dust, or I should say smoke, I returned to the house and went in search of a couple of aspirin, a cup of coffee, and Mary. The coffee and aspirin I found in the kitchen along with Billy, Tammie, and Sally.

Always the perfect hostess, Sally fixed me a small plate of sandwiches to go with the coffee and aspirin.

"Now, Jean," she informed me as she set

the items down on the granite countertop, "you're welcome to stay in here for as long as you want. That bunch in the dining room is enough to give anyone a headache, especially Kurt Summerfield. I don't know what it is exactly, but there's just something about him that makes my skin crawl. I don't trust him. And that Goody woman is all over the man. Why, I don't know. She's got to be young enough to be his daughter."

"Mom," said Billy, "maybe me and Tammie should stick around, at least until these people clear out of here. I don't like leaving you alone. For all we know, one of your paying guests could very well be a murderer, right, Mrs. Hastings?"

Before I could say yea or nay, Tammie spoke up. "Well, if you ask me, I think the gruesome twosome, Mr. M. and Ms R., had something to do with D. D.'s death."

"You mean Todd and Maxine?" I asked once I'd translated Tammie's verbal shorthand into conversational English.

"You got it, Mrs. H. I told Mrs. B. if I was her, I sure as heck would count the towels and the silverware before I'd let those two check out of here today."

"What makes you think they might have something to do with Dona Deville's death?" I asked, taking a bite of the most delicious chicken salad sandwich I'd ever tasted in my life.

"Because of what I heard her say to him when I was setting up the coffee urn on top of the console. I had to get down on the floor and practically crawl halfway under the darn cabinet to plug the pot in. I guess they didn't see me when they came up to the buffet. She says to him, she says, 'Like I told you, Todd, I'm a lot harder to get rid of than Dona, so don't you forget it.' Then he says to her, he says, 'How could I with you reminding me about it every chance you get.' Maybe they would have said more but Police Chief S. comes over and squats down right next me and asks if I needed help."

"Like they say, Tammie, timing is everything, and speaking of time," I said, "I've got to get going. There's a little something I need to take care of and Mrs. England will be going with me. We shouldn't be gone long. If it makes you feel any better, Billy, when we're done with our errand, we'll come back here and keep your mother company until everyone leaves."

"Thanks, Mrs. Hastings, I'd appreciate it," Billy said, looking relieved. "I've got another catering job to set up and Tammie's scheduled to work up at the club this afternoon. Neither one of us will be back 'til almost suppertime."

It was indeed time for me to leave. Thanking Sally for the coffee, Billy for the sandwich, Tammie for the info, and God for the aspirin, I went in search of Mary.

Seated in one of the beige and rose chenille upholstered morris chairs that formed a conversation area in the cozy living room, Mary was enjoying a bite-size fudge brownie, one of the several brownies that made up a pyramid of the dessert on her plate.

"Oh, Gin, you've got to try these little thingys. Billy made them himself and they're even better than the ones at the club, but don't tell Stella I said so. I wouldn't want to hurt her feelings or cause Billy any trouble, seeing that Stella's the top chef at the country club and Billy's her assistant. He says Stella's taught him so much, especially about baking. Here, try one."

Taking the tiny pastry from Mary, I tossed it into my mouth and washed it down with a swallow of ice tea from Mary's glass.

"Yeah, it was great. You about ready to leave?" Not waiting for an answer, I added, "I'll meet you in the car."

In addition to being a best friend and sister-in-law, Mary was also a problem. I didn't know how much, if anything, I should tell her. I certainly didn't want to alarm her but then again, she was a grown woman, and if she was going to come with me, she certainly should be made aware that we might possibly be putting ourselves in danger.

If things went the way that I thought they would, we would be in and out and back at Sally's before the murderer was even aware that I'd figured out the how and why of the elderly aunt's murder. Once that was accomplished, I would get in touch with Martha and give her the good news that I'd kept my part of the bargain. Then, with my nose back where it belonged, I'd be free to focus all my time and energy on my husband, whom I sorely missed. I was almost out of patience and notepaper and was seriously thinking of stopping by the hospital administrator's office. One of the quickest ways to spring someone out of a hospital is to hint that the patient's insurance has been depleted. It's amazing how that tiny bit of information can turn a two- to three-week stay into practically an overnighter.

The luncheon was still going with no signs of letting up soon. As I passed by Kurt Summerfield, he turned away. I had a sneaking suspicion that he, too, had been warned by Rollie Stevens about my sleuthing activities. I made sure that everyone, including the person who I truly believed to be the murderer, heard me tell Ellie that Mary and I were making a quick trip to Garrison General to bring Charlie a hot dog from Winnie's Weenie Wagon. I said the poor guy was sick of hospital food.

When Ellie heard that, she insisted on fixing a to-go box with enough sandwiches and brownies to feed Charlie and the entire nursing staff. She also came up with the bright idea that her fiancé, Peter, who was Charlie's primary doctor, could perhaps save me a trip because he had said something about having to run over to the hospital. But alas, the good doctor was nowhere to be found.

"My goodness," cried Ellie, "he was right here a minute ago. You don't suppose that he's disappeared like Vincent, do you, Mrs. Hastings?"

"I wouldn't worry about Peter. He's probably around here someplace. Maybe he stepped out in the yard for some fresh air or decided to walk off his lunch. But thanks anyway for the offer and for the box of goodies for Charlie. We're not going to be gone all that long."

CHAPTER TWENTY-NINE

"We're going where?" gasped Mary. "Did I hear you right? Tell me you didn't say Old Railway Road. My stars, why in the world do we want to go back there?"

"Would you have felt better if I said we were going to the Springvale mall?" I asked, lighting a cigarette and watching as the combination of speed and wind sucked the smoke out of the van.

The day was what we Hoosiers like to call a real scorcher, and seeing that I hadn't gotten around to getting the AC fixed, I had every window in the van wide open. Between the weather, the potholes, and the wind, Mary was more in danger of suffering from heat stroke, a concussion, or secondhand dust than from secondhand smoke. How she managed to hold on to the box that Ellie had fixed for me to supposedly bring to Charlie, much less open it without spilling a single crumb of brownie or glob of chicken salad, I'll never know. I was too busy driving like Danica Patrick to look at Mary.

"Of course I'd rather be going to the mall to shop than sleuthing with you. I have to be honest with you, Gin. This whole . . . whoooie! Now that was a pothole with a capital P. Anyway, like I was saying, this whole sleuthing business isn't as glamorous as I thought it was going to be. At least, not the way you do it. First you do a lot, and I mean a lot of talking to people, then you have these hunches or bouts of intuition or whatever you want to call them, then you go around annoying people and just when any normal person would call it quits, you go off on your own and eureka! You solve the crime."

"Jeez, Mar, what do you expect me to do? Run around like some hack writer's idea of a tough dame detective? Packin' heat, wearing five-inch heels, a tightly belted trench coat, and taking my wiskey neat? It would be interesting but I don't think very productive."

"Maybe not quite like that but it certainly wouldn't hurt if you patterned yourself a wee bit along . . . whoooie! My stars, Gin, slow down. One more bump like that and all this nice food is going to end up on the floor."

"Mary, would you please, please stick to what you were saying and leave the driving to me. And as far as where we are going and what we're going to do when we get there, it may seem dull to you but it is important. I need to see a couple of things for myself. Once I do that, I'm done and the ball will be in Rollie Stevens's court."

"Why him and not Matt?" Mary wanted to know. Her voice sounded muffled and I knew without looking at her that Mary had a mouthful of the brownie dessert.

"Because," I answered, steering the van around a hubcap that had fallen off somebody's car. I'd be willing to bet that car and cap were never reunited. Like socks, hubcaps lead a very independent life and think nothing of disappearing without notice. "Matt and Sid Rosen are working on a big hush-hush case; it's so hush-hush that even JR doesn't know anything about it except that it keeps Matt away from home a lot."

We were within a few feet of the driveway leading to the old cottage when Mary nearly choked on brownie crumbs.

"Gin, slow down. You're going to miss the turn," she screeched as the van whizzed down the road.

"Who said we were going to the cottage?

What I want to check out is down the road, like here," I said as I whipped the van into the parking area next to the defunct railway station. That's when I saw the remains of the chicken salad on the floor in front of Mary.

"Jeez, Mar, what a mess. I know the van's not the cleanest of vehicles, but chicken salad? When did that happen?"

"About three potholes ago. Don't blame me. You were the one driving. If you would have stopped by my house so that I could have picked up my purse, I'd be able to clean up the mess with a towelette. I always keep a supply of the little individual packets in my purse. Maybe you've got some in your emergency supply kit in your purse. Want me to look?"

"Don't bother, Mary. The only emergency supplies in my purse are two aspirin, a Band-Aid, an extra pack of cigarettes, and a couple of Midol tablets."

"Midol? Good grief, when was the last time you cleaned out your purse?"

I didn't bother to answer. Instead I grabbed a roll of white adhesive tape from the van's console and was almost across the road when Mary caught up with me.

"We drove all the way out here to stand by the interstate exit ramp? If you're waiting for someone, good luck," said Mary, scraping a mixture of mayonnaise and chicken from the bottom of one of her low-heel, black-patent leather pumps in a patch of nearby grass. "Almost everyone going to or coming from Seville uses the exit and entrance ramps on the other side of town. They're a heck of a lot closer to the business district and the college."

"I'm not waiting for anyone. I'm here to look at those," I said, pointing to the signs that stood formidably on each side of the exit ramp. The entrance ramp was located at the other end of the overpass that spanned Old Railway Road.

"Do me a favor, Mary. Read me exactly what those signs say, word for word. I think when you do, you'll have a renewed respect for my method of sleuthing."

Mary rolled her big, blueberry-colored eyes in exasperation. "Okay, here goes: DO NOT ENTER and DO NOT ENTER."

"Now, close your eyes," I instructed as I tore off two strips of the white tape and placed them on the signs. "Now, open your eyes and read me exactly what the signs say, word for word."

"ENTER and ENTER," gasped Mary. "Oh my stars, the signs! If someone messed with the signs to purposely trick Dona's elderly aunt into going the wrong way on the interstate, then her accident wasn't an accident at all."

"You got it, Mary," I answered as I removed the tape from the two signs. "The Washington Street sign was a prank. Stupid but still just a prank. What happened out here was as deliberate as it was deadly. In fact it was murderous."

"And it was done with tape?" Mary asked as we made our way back across the road to where the van was parked.

"It could've been done that way or perhaps the signs were temporarily removed. It could've been as simple as turning the signs around," I replied. "I think Vincent Salerno figured it out, which ultimately led to his disappearance."

"If that's the case, Gin, why didn't he report it to the police instead of disappearing?"

"Because the murderer stopped him before he had the chance. This entire case has been a series of connected incidences like that nursery rhyme, 'The House That Jack Built.' Do you remember it?"

"I'm not sure I can recall the entire thing," said Mary, "but didn't it go something like 'This is the house that Jack built and this is the mouse that lived in the house that Jack built.' Then it went on about the mouse that ate the cheese in the house and then the rat ate the mouse that ate the cheese and so on and so forth."

"And what did everything end up coming back to?" I asked, hoping that Mary would catch on to the analogy between the two murders and the nursery rhyme.

"Everything comes back to the house that Jack built," said Mary, "kind of like how everything comes back to Old Railway Road. Am I right, Gin?"

"Right on the button. Like I said, everything about this case is connected, beginning with the supposed accidental death of Dona's aunt and ending with the disappearance of Vincent Salerno. Everything starts and ends with Old Railway Road."

"Okay," said Mary, "I think I understand what you're saying, but what in the world was the killer's motive?"

"That, my dear Watson," I said, adapting the mannerism of Sherlock Holmes, the great fictional detective, "is what I hope to discover next at our last stop."

I was trying to lighten things up a bit for Mary's sake. The reality that not one but two murders had taken place on Old Railway Road horrified her. I knew she was anxious to leave the desolate area.

"You mean there's still more to do? Like what?" demanded Mary as we made our way back to the van.

"If you come with me, you'll see for yourself or you can wait for me here at the railroad station. It's entirely up to you, but trust me, it won't take long. I plan on being back at Sally's while the murderer is still enjoying Billy's fabulous food. By the way, Mar, you're right about the sandwiches being great."

Mary's natural curiosity made the decison for her. She was already in the van and buckled up before I put the key in the ignition.

Driving past the entrance to the old cottage, I turned down the rutted dirt and gravel side road, bringing the van to a halt behind the thick clump of trees that separated the cottage from the barn and shed. Before getting out of the van, I tooted the horn three times.

"What's with the horn, Gin? Are we meeting someone here?"

"No, in fact just the opposite," I said as I got out of the van. "If I'm right about what's in the barn or possibly in the shed, the last thing I want to do is to run into someone, especially the murderer. I figure if anyone was lurking about, the blasts from the horn would've sent them running out here to see who was making the racket and why."

Getting out of the van, I headed for the shed, the nearest of the two outbuildings.

"Hey, wait for me," cried Mary, unbuckling the seatbelt and scrambling to catch up with me.

The shed was locked, something I hadn't counted on. If it had been a movie or TV show instead of a real-life situation, I would've used some ingenuity and picked the lock.

"Jeez, now what?" I said more to myself than Mary, "I really need to see what's inside that shed."

"If that's the case, why don't you peek through the window?" Mary suggested. "It's pretty dirty but I think you could probably see something, maybe even what you want to see."

"From out of the mouths of babes," I said, grabbing Mary and pushing her toward the window.

"In case you haven't noticed, Gin, I haven't grown an extra six inches in the last few minutes. It's too high up. There's no way I can peek in that window."

"Me neither, but with your help, I think I can. Now lace your fingers together and give me a boost up."

After a couple of failed attempts, Mary managed to hang in there long enough for me to get a good look through the dirty windowpane. Other than a jumble of rusty garden tools, empty paint cans, and some broken bushel baskets, there wasn't anything of note to be seen. Disappointed and covered with grime from leaning against the window and side of the shed, I instructed Mary to follow me as I walked over to the barn.

The old barn, which dated back to the 1860s, had been repaired over the years by so many different people using so many different materials that little remained of the original structure.

"Cross your fingers, Mar, and say a prayer that the barn's not locked, otherwise we'll have to resort to plan B."

"Really? What's plan B?" Mary asked, still huffing from her stint as a human step stool.

I was saved from revealing the nonexistent plan by the carelessness of others. The lock on the door hadn't been properly secured, allowing access to the barn.

"Thank you, Saint Patrick," I said to the saint in charge of Irish luck.

Using two hands, I managed to pull open the heavy, reinforced oversized barn door, which Mary then promptly managed to pull closed as soon as we'd stepped inside.

"Good lord, Mary, I'm not a mole. Would you please open the damn door so I can find the light switch."

"Oh no, I can't get it to budge, not even an inch," wailed Mary. "If I didn't know better, I'd say that we're locked in. Maybe it's time for plan B."

Mary never did get the door opened and I never did find the light switch, but as my eyes became more accustomed to the semi-darkness of the barn (a few rays of light managed to sneak between the odd space here and there in the walls) I did find Abner Wilson's motive for murder — a fully operating meth lab. And last but not least, I found the investigator-cum-bodyguard, the missing Vincent Salerno.

CHAPTER
THIRTY

Trussed up like a calf in a rodeo, and with his mouth taped shut, "Just call me Vinny" had been tossed on the dirt floor in a section of the barn that, from the smell of it, had at one time housed farm animals. Aside from some nasty rope burns, and an assortment of bumps and bruises, Vincent Salerno was alive and for that I was grateful. So was Mary who had stumbled over him in the semidarkness and was on the verge of having another fainting spell.

"Mary Catherine Hastings England, don't you dare pass out. There's nothing available to toss in your face, not even dog water, unless you prefer that I use something from old man Wilson's handy-dandy, do-it-yourself pharmacy," I said, gesturing to the work bench that housed the paraphernalia used to make the horrific end product.

What I said to Mary, coupled with the fact that the insurance investigator was very much alive, snapped her out of it.

While a somewhat woozy Mary worked on freeing his hands and legs, I yanked the strip of masking tape from Salerno's mouth. Contrary to what I'd come to expect, thanks to Charlie's passion for action movies and TV shows, the first words out of the man's mouth were not those of gratitude but rather a collection of words and phrases that would've made even the most seasoned sailor blush. To his credit, once Salerno calmed down and rubbed his cheeks and mouth, his civil tongue returned and he thanked us properly for coming to his rescue.

Of course, once he started talking, he was almost impossible to shut up. He began by telling us that from the beginning Dona was convinced that her aunt, whose given name was Jenny, had been a victim of foul play.

After the authorities ruled the aunt's death an accident, the diet diva contacted the aunt's insurance company. The insurance company gave the job of looking into the accident to him, and Dona provided the cover he needed to conduct a covert investigation.

Dona was also convinced that whoever was behind the elderly woman's death was someone in her entourage. She believed that she and her daughter Ellie were next on the killer's list. Because she was popping prescription drugs like candy, she'd had become increasingly paranoid about it. But when she turned up dead, the investigator began having second thoughts about the aunt's death being a prank that went awry.

"Remember last Sunday when you asked me about my alibi for the time when Dona was murdered and I said I was following the advice of my horoscope?"

How could I forget, I thought while nodding my head in the affirmative and waiting for him to continue.

"Actually," he said, "I was nosing around the exit ramp by the old railroad station when Dona was murdered, something I wasn't about to admit because it put me in such close proximity to the scene of not one murder but two. I was afraid if you knew that then you would hinder my investigation with your amateur efforts to solve Dona's murder. I thought the warning I gave you about sticking to decorating would be enough to scare you off. I don't mind telling you, Mrs. Hastings, I'm sure glad I was wrong."

"But you still haven't explained how you ended up here," said Mary as we helped him to his feet.

We really needed to get out of there, so I suggested that Salerno save the rest of his explanation for the ride back to town. I assumed, that with the three of us pushing, the heavy barn door wouldn't be a problem. Unfortunately we were about to discover that the door was the least of our problems.

We were almost to the door when it suddenly swung open. The flood of light temporaily blinded us, making it impossible to determine if we had just been saved or captured by the person silhouetted in the doorway. The moment I heard the voice, I had the answer — and it wasn't good.

It was "Stanley Kowalski," the boy from the top floor of Abner Wilson's house, blocking our exit. He wasn't yelling for Stella but he was yelling for Abner Wilson. He also flipped on the light switch, the one I had been unable to find.

"Oh my stars, Gin," gasped Mary, "look at the shirt he's wearing. It's Herbie's bowling shirt, the one with his name on it. How do you suppose he got it?"

"Most likely the same way he gets everything he wants — he stole it. He probably got the gun he's holding the same way. It's kind of a nice touch. It gives his outfit that extra punch often lacking in your run-of-the-mill bowling attire."

"Hey, you with the big mouth and dirty clothes," he snarled at me, "for your info, I found this shirt in the alley behind our house. It was still in the box, not even opened. Me and Uncle Abner deal in drugs, not stolen goods. We leave that part of the business up to our customers and the fence over in Springvale. Now put a lid on it or I'll blow your friggin' head off."

Given such a narrow range of choices, I shut my mouth for the time being. The same couldn't be said of Mary, who lit into him as only someone who has raised a family of boys can do. Mary was really getting to the nasty punk, who seemed to be on the verge of at least letting her walk out of there, when Abner Wilson came limping into the barn.

In spite of knowing zilch about firearms, I couldn't help but notice that Abner Wilson's gun resembled the one Clint Eastwood was holding when he uttered the memorable movie line about a punk making his day. In contrast the gun that Stanley (his given name turned out to be Stanley) held in his hot little shaking hand looked just like the one Joan Crawford used in a lot of her films. She kept it in a tiny, clutch-type evening bag that had a huge diamond clasp. At exactly the right moment, she would open the purse and pull out the gun without ever removing her elbow length gloves. Her dexterity amazed me.

But I digress — my point being that Abner Wilson's gun was as big as Stanley's gun was small and both weapons were pointed in my direction.

"Well, well, if it ain't Miz Hastings and Miz England," said the old handyman in a manner that belied the seriousness of the situation. "Fancy meetin' you two ladies in a place like this. I see that you found what you was lookin' for."

"I guess you could say that, although I didn't expect to find Mr. Salerno in here. I must say, you were very convincing when you thanked me at the luncheon for delivering your message to him, telling him to stay away. I never thought that you were holding him captive in the barn."

"Surprised you, didn't I. Just like I did when I walked throught that door." Abner chuckled. "I bet you wish now that you went to the hospital like you said instead of snoopin' around this here barn. You think I swallowed that baloney about you runnin' up to the hospital to bring lunch to Mr. Hastings? Not me. After you left, I seen that young doctor fella walkin' around in the yard. I asked him how your husband was doin' and he tells me Charlie's under some kind of quarantine. No visitors. That's when I told Miz Birdwell I was feelin' poorly and took my leave, picked up my grandnephew Stanley at the house, and hightailed it out here."

Apparently, all that talk made Abner Wilson thirsty. Removing the flask from the back pocket of his overalls, he opened it and took a long drink. "With the profit we made on meth, me and Stanley are gonna live like a couple of kings south of the border."

"Lay off the booze, old man," ordered Stanley, "we got a lot of driving to do if we're going to make it to Mexico before the cops are onto us."

"Now don't you go a worryin' about the police. I talked to old Rollie Stevens after the funeral service," said Abner, taking another drink from the flask. "If he's onto anyone, it's that doctor fella. The smartest thing I did, aside from sending that old gal up that exit ramp, was havin' you swipe that heart listen' thing from the doctor's office while he was busy checkin' my bum leg. The only two on the whole dang Seville police force worth worrying about are Cusak and Rosen. Accordin' to Rollie Stevens they're at some kinda profilin' seminar being held up in Fort Wayne."

"I don't give a rat's ass what they're doing, I just want to get out of here and on our way before some of our customers either get caught by their parents for using meth or by the Springvale cops for fencin' the stuff they stole. Got that? Now lay off the booze while I get the rope." Stanley was halfway to the door when he turned around. "And stop talkin' to the one in the dirty clothes. She's got a big mouth and bad vibes."

"The feeling's mutual, chum," I called after the fast-retreating figure. Stanley was bad news but so far, unlike his great-uncle, he hadn't killed anyone.

With the blood of two people already on his hands, I knew that Abner Wilson was not about to set off to live like a king in Mexico with three witnesses for the prosecution merely tied up in the barn. No way, no how. The sunny side of the street was looking farther and farther away. If ever there was a time for plan B, this was it. Now all I had to do was think of something.

Apparently, Vincent Salerno was doing what I was doing but with more success. When Abner Wilson tipped the flask to his lips for another drink, the insurance investigator decided it was time to make his move. He rushed the old man and knocked him off his feet. Abner Wilson grabbed Salerno's leg and soon the two were locked in a wrestling match. Shouting for Mary and me to make a run for it as the old handyman shoved his face into the dirt floor, Salerno didn't see Abner reaching for the gun that had fallen out of his hand when the younger man knocked him down. Salerno also didn't see the returning Stanley who, with gun drawn, blocked our exit from the barn. When the big gun hit him in the back of his head, Vincent Salerno didn't see anything at all. He was unconscious.

Using the steel tip of his work shoe, the murderous Abner pushed the limp body of the investigator into the stable area, where it came to rest in front of an ancient, battered storage bin that was about the size of a large packing crate. My guess was that at one time the bin was used for animal feed but like everything else in the old barn, including the meth lab, it had outlived its usefulness.

"God damn," said Abner Wilson to no one in particular, "that investigative fella smells worse than that old horse stall and that's sayin' somethin'. I swear that whole floor back in the stall area is ninety-nine percent horse manure and one percent dirt."

"Yeah, I agree with you on that," said Stanley, breaking into a sly grin and showing teeth almost as black as his stringy hair. Obviously, Stanley had been as hooked on meth as Abner was on making money from it. Neither activity requires a very high IQ. "I think that stall's the perfect place for a couple of snoopy broads, especially the big-mouth one."

"Well then, why don't you herd them in there and tie them up tight while I go get that container of gasoline from the back of the truck?" the old man replied as he retrieved his flask from the top of a pile of trash.

Upon finding that all the liquor had trickled out, Abner Wilson limped over to where the insurance investigator lay pressed against the storage bin. Then he stopped short and turned away.

"He ain't worth the bullet. The fire will take care of him along with everything else in this old barn," he said as he began making his way toward the barn door.

"You mean you're not fixing to take any of the lab stuff with us? Hell, there's more than enough room in that investigator guy's SUV. I say we take it with us," said Stanley as he began pushing me and Mary into the stinking stall area.

"You know somethin', Stanley, sometimes you're as dumb as a stump. That's all we need is to get caught haulin' around that stuff. Use your head. When we get ready to set up another lab, we can replace all that equipment as easy as pie."

"Even in Mexico?" replied the agitated Stanley, poking the small gun into Mary's back in an effort to hurry her along.

"Yeah, sure. They got hardware stores, drugstores, and supermarkets same as us. And if they don't, we'll just cross the border back into the States and go to a Wal-Mart superstore. They got everything, like they say, including lower prices."

"Okay then. You get the gasoline and I'll get these two ready for toasting. See, Unc, you're not the only one who can make a joke." Stanley was immensely pleased with himself.

With Abner Wilson fetching the gasoline from the back of his battered pickup truck, Stanley ordered Mary and me to sit back-to-back on the floor with arms behind us and legs drawn up to our knees. We did as we were told, which led to the first of Stanley's problems.

The twentysomething Stanley couldn't manage to tie both of us up at the same time. He also couldn't figure out how to tie even one of us up while keeping the other at bay without letting go of either the gun or the rope. It would have been funny except the spot we were in was no laughing matter.

My offer to hold the gun for him was met with a resounding no, but Mary reminded him that Abner was not going to be pleased with him should he return with the gasoline to find that Stanley had failed to do as he was told. Since Mary seemed to have a better rapport with Stanley than I did, I kept quiet and let her do the talking. He finally agreed to her suggestion that he hold the gun while she tied me up. Once that was done, he could then tie up Mary, who was, in her own words, a very trustworthy person.

"You know, Stanley, it hurts me to see the way your uncle talks down to you," clucked Mary, keeping up a steady stream of motherly comments as she bound my ankles tightly before starting on my wrists, which were behind my back, "but I'm very proud of the way you hold your temper. It can't be easy working for a man like Abner. For one thing, he's so much older than you that he doesn't seem to understand where you're coming from. Do you know what I'm saying? I'll bet he even complains about your music, something I know from having raised my own sons is terribly important."

Mary then proceeded to rattle off names

of recording artists that for the most part were unknown to me, except for the ones that had made headlines with behavior often described by the media as being lewd, obscene, or unlawful. I couldn't have been more surprised if Mary had ripped open her blouse and revealed a tattoo of Herman's Hermits on her ample bosom. But like I said, I kept my mouth shut except for a few loud shrieks of faux pain as Mary tied the ropes around my wrists.

By the time old man Wilson returned with the gasoline and a snootful of liquor, Mary and I sat back-to-back tied up and, as Stanley had so comically put it, ready for toasting.

With Stanley busy pouring gasoline around the outside perimeter of the barn, I took a last shot at asking the drunken Abner a couple of questions such as what had changed in his life that led to not one but two murders.

In words that were as slushy as they were slurred, Abner said that he made more money with the meth lab in six months than he did in six years of washing walls, painting fences, picking up trash, and repairing lawn mowers. He also said that after almost twenty years of mailing his rent check for the shed and barn to a woman he'd never met and who had never been out to the property, she notified him via mail that she was coming out to inspect the cottage and had plans to turn the place into a weekend retreat, something that would've put a definite crimp in his lucrative drug business.

"I thought by gettin' rid of the old lady, I'd be back where I started, mailin' my rent check to her next of kin, that Dona woman. Never thought she'd turn out to be nuttier than a fruitcake and have bigger plans for the property than the old biddy aunt had. I had no choice but to get rid of her, too. She was going to have me thrown off the property by the police. I couldn't let that happen."

Abner Wison paused and raised the refilled flask to his lips. He kept it there until it was empty once again. Totally inebriated, he struggled to continue and I struggled to make sense of what he was saying. What I gathered from his slurred speech was that thanks to Hilly Murrow's newsy news reports he was aware of some trouble between Peter Parker and Dona Deville.

Donna called Abner at his house on Fourth Street Friday morning to inform him that she would be out to inspect the property after the book signing. Abner wasn't home and she ended up speaking with Stanley. When asked by Dona to give Abner the message, Stanley told her in no uncertain terms to stay the hell away from the barn and shed.

When Dona heard that, she was furious and told Stanley to tell his uncle that if he didn't meet her at the cottage by seven fifteen Saturday morning, all hell was going to break loose. Abner got the message and was ready and waiting for Dona, stethoscope in hand.

CHAPTER
THIRTY-ONE

It's been said that in the moments before you die, your whole life flashes before your eyes. The only thing that flashed before my eyes was the sight of Dumb and Dumber, the pet names I'd secretly assigned to Abner Wilson and his nephew, Stanley, running out of the barn after a heated arguement between the two over where to light the fire. Stanley favored the inside of the barn. His logic was that that way they would be sure that we hadn't gotten free and put the fire out. The drunken Abner argued for the outside and ultimately prevailed. The reason they raced out of the barn was to move the SUV from its hiding place against the barn's outside rear wall.

Almost as soon as they locked the barn door on their way out, I'd freed myself and was busy untying Mary. It was when I was struggling with a particularly stubborn knot that we both heard the unmistakeable whoosh of gasoline igniting. Again the luck of the Irish was with us and the knot released just as the first signs of smoke began to seep into the barn, along with the heat from the now-growing fire.

Pulling my cotton half-slip down around my feet, I took it off and tore it into strips which we then used as face masks against the smoke. In the pile of trash where Abner's liquor had landed I found a dirty but damp rag that smelled of whiskey. Dropping down to the floor, Mary and I crawled over to Vincent Salerno, who was in the process of regaining consciousness. I thrust the whiskey-soaked rag into his face and tied it to his nose and mouth area using a strip of my slip.

I was out of ideas and I knew from the heat and smoke that we were running out of time. Hoping for a miracle, I began to pray and was unaware that in my desperation, I'd raised my voice until Vincent Salerno added a solemn amen to my prayers. Expecting Mary to do the same, I was confused when her expected amen turned into a hello. My cell phone! Mary had my cell phone!

Snatching it from her hand, my own hand was shaking so badly that I dropped the phone on the floor. In the semidarkness,

Stanley had dutifully shut the light off when he exited the barn, and hampered by the choking smoke, heat, and noise of the fire, I ran my hand over the area where I thought the phone might have landed.

"Oh God, please help me find the phone." I wasn't praying; I was shouting. When both my companions told me to shut my big mouth, I was so taken aback that I did just that. That's when Vincent Salerno passed the phone to Mary and she in turn passed it to me.

"It's for you, Gin, I think it's JR," Mary managed to gasp before almost being overcome by a coughing fit brought on by the increasing smoke.

"JR, we need help. Call nine-one-one and tell them fire. The old barn by the cottage. Railway Road. Save us," I shouted into the phone or at least I thought I did until I listened to JR's response.

"Mother, I gotta go. Kerry's late for her ballet lesson," said JR using a rapid-fire delivery, something she does when she is especially irritated with me. "I can't understand a word you're saying when you cough like that, Mother. You really ought to give up smoking. Check your phone messages. I left you one about the underground tunnel that runs from the barn to the railroad station. Catch you later." And with that JR, supermom, was gone.

Handing the phone to Mary, I asked her to call 911 for help after making sure that she, unlike JR, understood. Then turning to Vincent Salerno, and in a voice that sounded more like Walter Cronkite than me, I asked him to help me find the tunnel. JR is her father's daughter. She never fibs. If she said there was a tunnel, you can bet your life on it. And that is exactly what I was doing with not just one life but three.

Mary was still talking to the 911 operator, who insisted that Mary stay on the line 'til help arrived, when I looked into the bin and discovered the tunnel entrance hidden beneath a couple of layers of filth and debris along with not one but two false bottoms.

With me leading the way, Vincent Salerno in the middle, and Mary bringing up the rear, still talking to the 911 operator, we hunched over and made our way through the long and very dark tunnel. Along the way I suspected that we had company of the rodent variety with very long tails and sharp teeth, but I kept that information to myself. I wasn't sure if my back or my nerves were going to give out first, but by the time we'd reached the trap door hidden beneath the floor of the railroad station's baggage room, the three of us, survivors all, looked, smelled, and acted as if we'd just returned from an extended stay in the wilds of Borneo.

When Matt, accompanied by Sid Rosen, found us in a heap on the floor of the station's waiting room, he smiled and said, "Jean Hastings, party of three, your table's ready."

"Smoking or nonsmoking?" I managed to ask before being whisked off to Garrison General Hospital along with Mary and Vincent Salerno. Incidentally, "Just call me Vinny" turned out to be a really nice guy. So much for first impressions.

CHAPTER THIRTY-TWO

The following morning I awoke to a note that had been left on the bedside table in my hospital room. The note simply read: *If you need me, just whistle.* It was unsigned but like the notes I'd been leaving for Charlie, no signature was needed. I knew who'd sent it and understood the message.

Feeling like the drunk who sobers up in jail but then wonders when his freedom will be restored, I pressed the call button in hopes of getting the answer. Instead, all I got was a scolding from the head nurse, who informed me that the button was only to be used to summon help.

Since my vital signs were in the normal range, she ordered me to get back under the covers, turned on her heel, and bustled out of the room. As far as when I could expect to be released, I was in the same spot as the drunk — I didn't know.

After failing to glean any information

regarding my status from the student nurse who took my temperature, the aide who delivered my breafast tray, the hospital chaplain who dropped by to say hello, and an intern who had me confused with another patient, I gave up. Whoever said that you can't fight city hall must have been in the hospital at the time.

I later leaned from the cleaning lady that Peter Parker had been in to see me when I was asleep. She overheard him tell Charlie, who was present at the time, that I was scheduled to be released the following day.

The woman was a virtual fount of information. She said that Mary had been released the night before after receiving a clean bill of health. She even knew that Denny was with Mary the entire time Mary was in the emergency room and that Salerno was up on the third floor (I was on the second floor) in room 321, Charlie's room. Because of the concussion he'd suffered, Salerno was going to be in for a while, doctor's orders.

"But how can he share a room with Charlie? Doesn't my husband have some kind of unidentified, deadly rash?"

"Listen, dearie, it was much to do about nothing. He had a bad case of prickly heat. Yesterday I brought him a bottle of calamine lotion from Finklestein's and he's as good as new," said the cleaning lady as she headed for the door. "That hubby of yours is a real prince of a fella. He insisted on paying me five bucks for the lotion. See ya later." And with that said, she was gone.

Without a clock or watch, I turned on the TV in an effort to keep track of the time. The soaps were on all the network channels so I knew I'd missed the noon news out of Indy.

Switching channels, I stopped when I hit our local channel. Hilly Murrow was about to come on with what the voice-over called a special report. Assuming it would be about what had happened the day before out on Old Railway Road, I sat back and waited.

Alas, the entire report, except for a blurb about "a suspicious barn fire out in the boondocks," centered on the Dona Deville funeral service, the luncheon, and the people in attendance. I was singled out by our ace reporter for wearing, as she put it, "an inappropriate, skimpy T-shirt, play shoes, and a see-through cocktail skirt." When she was commenting on my outfit, the expression on her pinched face reflected her obvious disapproval.

"Yo, Miss Manners," I hissed at the image on the TV screen, "I'm an interior designer, not Coco Chanel. And for your information, I was wearing a cotton half-slip."

Disgusted, I switched to HGTV and watched as a talented interior designer transformed a small, narrow, outdated bathroom into a large, updated, and functional master bath.

By knocking out the wall between an unused hall closet and the bathroom's linen closet, needed footage was added to the width of the room. Newly installed can lights and a skylight illuminated the entire space and rid it of its previous cavelike atmosphere.

Since the homeowners preferred showering rather than bathing, the tub and shower unit was removed and replaced with a large walk-in shower. The new shower area was tiled from floor to ceiling in large, chocolate-brown ceramic tiles and trimmed midway around in small, multicolored accent tiles.

Double sinks with brushed chrome fixtures were installed along with new hickory wood cabinets. The granite countertop that the homeowners, with help from the designer, had selected was basically a sandy color with streaks of cream, green, and chocolate brown. Over the sinks were twin mirrors with narrow forest-green frames.

Because the husband was a very tall man,

the designer raised the height of the counter, something that the man greatly appreciated. The happy homeowners were oohing and aahing over their new master bath when Rollie Stevens walked into my hospital room. The way my luck was running, I wouldn't have been surprised if he'd come to arrest me for not wearing black to Dona Deville's funeral.

"Afternoon, Mrs. Hastings. Mind if I sit down?" he asked as he pulled the bedside chair away from the head of the bed and moved it toward the foot.

"Be my guest," I answered with a smile. Uncertain why he'd dropped in on me, I kept quiet and waited for him to continue speaking.

"I know it's your line of business and all, but I would appreciate it if you'd shut off that decorator program or at least turn it down. This darn new hearing aid picks up everything. If I thought I could get away with it, I'd take it out and pretend I lost it."

I knew he was going somewhere with his remarks. With patience, I figured I'd eventually find out exactly where. In the meantime, I used the remote and turned off the TV.

"But you know my Martha, she'd probably run right out and buy me a new one. She got this thing about helping me.

262

'Course I'm not telling you anything you don't already know, right, Jean? I'll call you Jean and you can call me Rollie, okay?"

"No problem, Rollie. How is Martha? I haven't talked to her lately, or Charlie either for that matter. According to what young Dr. Parker tells me, she's doing a great job getting Charlie up and moving."

"Yeah, she's a heck of a therapist," said Rollie, shifting his stocky body in the too-small, uncomfortable chair. The police chief looked so ill at ease, I decided to end his misery by cutting to the chase.

"Okay, Chief," I said, addressing him by his official title, which was a signal that I wasn't buying his friendly banter and wanted to get to why he'd stopped by to see me. "How much do you know and how did you figure it out?"

"Let's just say that after being married over fifty years to the same woman, there's not much I don't know about Martha and she don't know about me," said the police chief, looking as though the weight of the world had just been removed from his shoulders.

"When I started complaining about all hours she was spending with your husband, she clammed up and let me rant and rave. That's not normal for someone who's as feisty as Martha. Did you know she even stood up to that Castro fella? In public, no less. He tried to get her to back down but she wouldn't do it. Instead, she went to his brother and got him to sneak her out of the country. Now that's what I call feisty. Of course the brother denied the whole thing."

In an effort to keep Rollie Stevens on track, I asked him how he got Martha to tell him the whole story. So far, neither one of us had used the word "deal," but I knew the conversation was leading up to it.

"I'm embarrassed to say this, him being your husband and all, but when I couldn't get anything out of Martha I felt something wasn't right," said Rollie, "so I stopped by to see Charlie. He's a heck of a guy, but I guess you know that already."

I nodded my head, smiled broadly, and waited for Rollie Stevens to continue.

"We had a good long talk about this that and the next thing, you know, stuff I don't think I have to explain, but at any rate when we got to talking about the Dona Deville murder, Charlie yells 'Bingo' so loud, the head nurse come in and gave us both a lecture. He figured out the whole thing for me. I went home and never said a word to Martha. It would've ruined everything because everything she did was for me."

I waited while the police chief removed a neatly folded, clean, white handkerchief from the inside pocket of his uniform jacket and wiped the tears that threatened to run down his gingerbread-colored cheeks.

"Darn allergies," he said, clearing his throat and pulling a small tape recorder from the right-hand pocket of his jacket. "Now, what have you got for me?"

An hour later, and after giving him my word of honor that I would never tell Martha that the secret deal I'd made with her wasn't a secret to Rollie or Charlie, the police chief kissed me on my cheek (that really suprised me) and said good-bye.

Maybe because I had given him a tape recorder full of information, he felt I deserved some information in return. I don't know that for sure, but for whatever reason, before he took his leave, he explained that the hush-hush investigation Matt had been conducting tied in with the whole Deville/Wilson business. While I was busy with the Deville investigation, Matt and Sid Rosen, with the police chief's knowledge and blessing, were hot on the trail of the meth lab and its connection to the rash of buglaries and car break-ins that Seville had been experiencing. The robberies and break-ins were being done by Abner's young customers who needed money to fund their drug habit. They took most of what they stole to a fence in Springvale.

I was delighted that Rollie Stevens decided to share the information with me because after I had time to think about all that had happened the day before, it had puzzled me that it was my son-in-law, Matt, who had been on hand to greet me at the railroad station. Until Rollie Stevens explained how Matt's investigation dovetailed with mine, I hadn't realized the two investigations were even remotely connected.

After Rollie had departed, I was seriously thinking of making a run to the third floor to see Charlie, but I didn't think I'd be able to get away with running around the halls of the hospital dressed in a skimpy hospital gown. With my luck I'd run into Hilly Murrow and be publicly taken to task for running around in an obscene nightgown. My problem of how to get to Charlie's room and what to wear was solved when my husband came walking, or rather hobbling, through the door.

"Hi, sweetheart. Want some company?" he said, sitting himself down in the little chair that Rollie Stevens had so recently vacated.

"You better believe it, especially if it's

you," I replied, hopping out of bed and giving Charlie a kiss and hug. "Good lord, Charlie, we've been like two ships passing in the night," I said as I plopped down on the edge of the bed. "I like your robe and pajamas. Are they new?"

"Yeah, JR surprised me with them yesterday afternoon, but we can talk about that later. What we need to talk about right now is what landed you in the hospital. And before you begin with your explanation, I think I should warn you that I've already talked to Matt."

While Charlie wasn't exactly his old jolly self, at least he seemed to be reasonably calm.

"Jeez, I almost don't know how or where to begin," I said, knowing I had to proceed with the utmost caution. My amateur sleuthing has been a thorn in Charlie's side from day one. If I wasn't careful, the all too familiar lecture about me sticking my nose into other people's business, especially police business, could reach a new level.

"I suggest that you start at the beginning with you and Mary discovering Dona Deville's body and ending with you, Mary, and my new roommate hopping the underground express to the old railroad station," Charlie instructed, "and don't leave anything out, including why you made that deal with Martha Stevens."

Trapped and with nowhere to go, I did as I was told. When I got to the part about being tied up in the burning barn, I tried to put a positive spin on the incident, which was virtually impossible.

". . . and then I woke up and read your note. It was as clever as it was sweet," I said, flashing what I hoped was a winning smile and steeling myself for Charlie's lecture.

Like a prosecuting attorney delivering the closing arguement in a slam-dunk case, Charlie hit on all the mistakes I'd made and the dire consequences that followed, such as not going to the police and ending up in a burning barn. He also reminded me that if he didn't love me so much, he wouldn't care that I had developed "a taste for solving deadly puzzles."

I was saved from giving Charlie my word that I would give up sleuthing by the appearance of Martha Stevens, who was there to escort Charlie back to his room via the wheelchair she'd brought along. She flashed me the okay sign for keeping my part of our deal as she settled Charlie in the chair and wheeled him out of the room.

Later that evening, the nursing staff arranged for me and Charlie to have a candlelight dinner in my room. All was forgiven, and like my investigation, it ended on a positive note.

Chapter
Thirty-Three

The next morning, I called JR. Even though it was seven o'clock, I knew that she would be up and dressed.

"Hi, Mom, I figured I'd be hearing from you this morning. How was your dinner last night?"

"Jeez, I know news travels fast in this town but I never thought it traveled quite that fast. How did you find out about it. Was it in Hilly Murrow's column in today's paper?" I was being sarcastic. Either JR didn't realize that or she chose to ignore my behavior.

"No, as a matter of fact, last night we got a sitter for the kids and Matt took me out to dinner at Milano's. We ran into Peter and Ellie. Your little date with Pops was their idea and the nurses helped them to pull it off," giggled JR. "Ellie wanted to include some dance music but Peter nixed that. He didn't think that was a very good idea with

Pops's cast and all. Not to change the subject, but what's on your mind besides me bringing you some clean clothes when I pick you up later this morning? Peter said you'd be released probably somewhere around ten."

"A couple of things, starting with your phone call to me when I was fighting for my life in a burning barn, and what happened to my van? It has my purse in it. I also want to know how Pesty managed to survive without both me and your father."

"That's more than a couple of things," JR said before informing me that because of my keeping her on the phone, she'd pushed the wrong button on the microwave oven and instead of keeping Matt's breakfast warm, "the microwave burnt it up. We can talk after I get you home. Love ya, bye."

Three long hours later, I was in JR's pickup truck and on my way home. Kettle Cottage never looked so good.

Before collecting me at the hospital, JR had brought Pesty back from her house and given the pampered little Kees fresh water and breakfast. When Pesty saw me come through the back door and into the kitchen, she ran to greet me with enthusiasm generally saved for French fries and cheese sticks.

With the exception of Charlie not being

home, things seemed pretty normal. Thanks to Matt, my car keys and purse were on the counter and the van was parked in the driveway.

Over a plate of Mrs. Fields chocolate chip cookies and glasses of milk, JR told me all about her connection with the underground tunnel that saved my life and the lives of Mary and Vincent Salerno.

"Remember last Monday when you had me and Aunt Mary over to discuss your investigation," said JR, who continued as I nodded my head, "and we ended up talking about the twins going on the field trip to the railroad station and I mentioned that as a kid I took the exact same trip?"

"Yes, I do," I said, "the one I missed because of Herbie Waddlemeyer's big, fat head."

"Mother, please, let's not go into that again. You're beginning to sound like Grandma Kelly. Pretty soon you'll be telling me how tough you had it during the Depression."

"JR, for your information I wasn't even born until after the Great Depression was long over, and since moving to California after Grandpa died, your grandmother seems to have forgotten all about it. Now all she talks about is whale watching, saving the sharks, and surfing. Did I tell you how she wants to be pushed out to sea on her boogie board when she dies? She's got the whole thing planned . . ."

"As I was saying," said JR, rolling her eyes and running over my last sentence, "Sally Birdwell was our guide and because of her, I developed an interest in Overbeck pottery. It bugged me because I couldn't remember why, but in my mind the pottery had some connection or other with Dona Deville's property, which in turn was connected to her murder. You know what I'm saying?"

I nodded my head and once again thought about the nursery rhyme with all the connections.

"Remember I said to you a couple of times that if I thought of anything, even if it seemed trivial, I would let you know? Well, when Matt felt so bad about me having to be both mom and dad to the twins 'cause he was so tied up with his investigation, he surprised me with another Overbeck figurine to add to my collection."

"What does that have to do with the tunnel? You are going to explain the connection, aren't you?" I said, wishing I could light up a cigarette. Because of JR's pregnancy and since we were sitting inside and not outside, I decided to curtail my smoking for the time being.

"I'm getting to it, and I'd get there faster if you'd stop interrupting me," replied JR as she helped herself to the last cookie on the plate.

"My new little figurine is a depiction of one of the many slaves that traveled the Underground Railroad provided by the abolitionists in the days before and during the Civil War. Sally not only told us all about the railroad, she also showed us a portion of it when she opened the hidden door beneath the racks once used to store things in the baggage room.

"At the time, most of the kids were bored or disappointed when they found out that there wasn't an actual set of tracks or a train in the tunnel. They were even more disappointed when Sally told them that they couldn't check out the other end of the tunnel that was hidden in the horse stall because the barn was on private property."

"You know," I said, "I've read about the Underground Railroad but I never knew that there was one in this area. And to think it saved me just like it saved the lives of people whose only crime was that they wanted to be free and treated like human beings and not property."

"When I held the new little figurine in my

hand," said JR, looking close to tears, "I thought of all the slaves that didn't make it. I really don't quite understand it myself, but all of a sudden I had this terrible urge to tell you about the tunnel. It was so compelling that I left you three messages on your regular phone."

"I was at the funeral and luncheon. When I stopped by the house after the funeral to check on Pesty, I never thought to check for messages."

"I was afraid of that, and like I said, it was so weird how I couldn't shake the feeling it was imperative that I tell you about the tunnel that day. So I kept calling you and calling you on your cell phone. When Aunt Mary finally answered it, I was more than a bit irritated with you. I had no idea where you were or what was happening."

"And with all that was happening, I forgot that Mary had my cell phone in her pocket, and she didn't remember it either until the wad of Kleenex she had in her pocket shifted when she all but collapsed on the floor of the horse stall. That's when she felt the phone vibrating."

JR went to the pantry and helped herself to the last of the cookies. "What?" she said as she caught me smiling at her. "After all, I am eating for two."

Reaching into the box of diet doggy treats, she gave one to Pesty, who'd dashed over to the pantry in hopes of getting a cookie, not a dog treat. Giving JR a look of disgust, she dropped the treat from her mouth and retreated to her spot under the kitchen table.

Clutching the little stack of cookies to her chest, JR was about to sit down again when she mentioned that while she and Ellie were talking at Milano's, the subject of the old cottage came up.

"She asked me if Designer Jeans would be interested in taking on the job of redoing the cottage. Of course, I said yes. And get this, Mom, she says she's leaving everything, even the budget, up to us."

Leaping out of my chair, I embraced JR in a bear hug, showering Pesty, who'd peeked out from beneath the table to see what all the excitement was about, with cookie crumbs.

"Mother, you just broke my cookies!" JR said, sounding like a little girl again.

"And you, my darling daughter," I replied, sounding like a very happy interior designer, "just made my day!"

Ellie told JR that she felt both her mother and her aunt had lost their lives attempting to turn the cottage into a useful, comfy abode.

"Ellie and Peter want to redo the cottage as a tribute to Aunt Jenny and Dona," said JR.

Removing a small packet from her purse, JR showed me some of the pictures that Ellie had selected from various country living magazines. While none of the photographs depicted exactly the decor that Ellie wanted, they provided a starting point.

Three hours later, JR and I had decided on a proposal to present to Ellie regarding the makeover of the cottage. Our plan was to combine the old with the new. In keeping with the spirit of American country, which reflects American individualism, we would work closely with Ellie so that her personality would be the driving force in picking colors, fabrics, and accessories throughout the house. She'd already told JR that she favored stainless-steel appliances for the kitchen and hoped that they could be combined with country furniture and accessories.

"And the best part of the whole thing," said JR, "is that her aunt Jenny left Ellie an entire house of antiques in Indianapolis. Ellie said even though she hadn't been to the aunt's house in years, she remembers seeing things such as a trestle table, a grandfather clock, rocking chairs, dry sinks, sleigh beds, and quilts. Lots and lots of quilts. You know, Mom, I think that between Designer Jeans and Aunt Jenny's antiques, we can give Ellie the home she's always wanted."

"And you know something, JR, I think you're right," I answered. And she was.

Because of Aunt Jenny's penchant for saving everything from skeins of yarn, buttons, old hatboxes, teapots, and baskets to kitchen implements of wire, JR and I had no problem finding appropriate accessories for the cottage. Our only real challenge was the kitchen. While the two upstairs bedrooms and bathroom, like the downstairs living room, dining room, and half bath, were easily turned into real country charmers, the kitchen with its sleek stainless steel appliances presented us with the problem of how to blend old with new.

After considering a variety of countertops, we settled for poured concrete in a light rosy beige, which complemented the diamond-patterned painted wood floor of creamy beige and faded red. We at first considered open cabinetry but found it made the walls of the kitchen a bit too busy, so we switched to cherry wood cabinetry with solid doors and recycled hardware pulls and handles. We used cherry-stained beadboard on the walls and around the sides of the oversized kitchen island. The top of the island was done in stainless steel, which helped to bridge the old with the new. As with the other rooms of the house, Ellie picked the accessories that reflected her likes and not ours.

Because of JR's pregnancy, we switched roles, with me doing most of the grunt work and JR handling things such as trips with Ellie to fabric stores, flea markets, and garage sales. In the process of doing so, JR and Ellie formed a close and enduring friendship. I like to think that Aunt Jenny and Dona would have been pleased with Ellie's decision to turn the old cottage into a splendid example of an American country home.

EPILOGUE

Charlie was released from the hospital the following week, and because of the close bond he'd developed with Martha Stevens, she made regular visits to Kettle Cottage to check on his progress once the cast was removed. Because of Dr. Peter Parker's skill as a surgeon and Martha's skill as a physical therapist, Charlie was back hacking away on the golf course long before Sleepy Hollow closed it for the season.

To celebrate Charlie's release, Matt and JR hosted another terrific backyard barbecue and invited half of Seville, including Herbie Waddlemeyer, who was still mourning the loss of his bowling shirt — the one with his name on it — to welcome Charlie home.

Sally Birdwell used the occassion of the barbecue to announce that the Birdwell house was now a licensed and certified bed-and-breakfast inn. Billy used the occasion to pass out cards for his new catering business. And last but not least, Ellie and Peter Parker used the occasion to announce that they would be getting married just as soon as Doc and Lucy returned from their vacation in Hawaii.

The twins were on hand, of course, and were very excited that a baby brother or sister would be joining the Cusak clan in December. When the kids were out of hearing range, Matt filled in some of the blanks regarding the Deville/Wilson investigation, as it came to be known. He revealed that the Seville police arrived on the scene expecting to conduct a raid on the meth lab and take Abner and Stanley into custody. What they found instead was the barn ablaze and the two criminals making a break for it in Salerno's SUV.

With Matt and Sid Rosen in hot pursuit, the drunken Abner lost control of the SUV, smashing it into a tree. Neither Abner or Stanley had bothered to buckle up and were pronounced dead at the scene of the accident.

The fire department arrived too late to save the barn, which was a shame given the old structure's history as a stop on the Underground Railroad.

Matt recognized my van parked by the

clump of trees and thought for sure that I had perished in the barn fire but thanks to the 911 operator, who contacted Rollie Stevens, who then contacted Matt, he was sent on to the railroad station where he heard our feeble cries for help.

The town council was so impressed with Rollie Stevens's handling of the case, they voted to give him a raise. Needless to say, the elderly police chief did not retire, much to his wife's dismay.

Ellie was the only one of Dona's entourage who decided to put roots down in Seville. She had generously signed most of the real estate she'd inherited from her mother over to her father, who didn't waste any time getting back to Indy and in touch with a certain multimullionaire. The only piece of real estate she kept was the old cottage that Aunt Jenny had specifically left to Dona, who in turn left it to Ellie.

Vincent Salerno, who eventually made a full recovery, returned to Columbus, Ohio, the home of his employer, and was soon off investigating another questionable accident. He stopped at Kettle Cottage on his way out of town to thank me for being, as he put it, "one snoopy broad."

No one in Seville seemed to know or care what happened to Maxine Roberts, Todd

Masters, or Marsha Gooding. I think that Hilly Murrow unknowingly said it best when she mentioned the trio's departure on her TV news report. She shook her head sadly and said that the people of Seville would probably never see the likes of them again. So far, so good.

A FEW WORDS ABOUT COUNTRY STYLE

To begin with, unlike other decors such as Art Deco, art nouveau, contemporary, and modern, country style is not one style but several styles such as English, French, American, and Tuscan. Tuscan country is currently enjoying immense popularity in the United States.

One of the nicest things about country style is that it is eclectic and allows you to borrow from other areas. For instance, you can decorate a kitchen with a stenciled backsplash, painted open shelving, a maple trestle table, mismatched ladder-back chairs, textured walls, and an arrangement of apples or oranges in a Depression glass bowl you inherited from your grandmother, and you've got yourself a country kitchen that borrows from all of the country styles mentioned above.

So start looking around and go to that garage sale down the street or drive over to the flea market next weekend. You may or may not find exactly the accent or furniture piece you want to add to your country decor, but you may find that you enjoyed meeting a lot of nice folks. Remember, above all, country is never formal. It's mix and match with ease and simplicity.

PAINTING TIPS

No matter what decor you settle on for your home, chances are unless you plan on paneling or wallpapering every room in your home, something that was popular in the 1960s, you're going to end up painting. Here's a few things I've learned over the years that I think you'll find helpful in your next painting project:

Consider using a coat of high-quality primer on the walls, especially if you're painting over a strong color with a softer color. It could save you from applying a second coat of paint.

Do not, and I repeat, do not paint when you are tired or if you've got a house full of unruly children under the age of twelve.

When you are painting don't plan on cooking anything. Either make yourself a PB and J sandwich, order in, or eat out. If you eat out, go to a dimly lit restaurant because chances are you're going to have paint in your hair, on your fingernails, on your clothing.

If you're pregnant, I suggest you either get someone else to do your painting or postpone doing it yourself until after the birth of your baby.

Never paint without proper ventilation, good lighting, drop cloths for furniture and floors, and plenty of clean rags.

Be careful when using masking tape. It isn't foolproof and you could end up with a mess should the paint bleed through the tape. Also, sometimes masking tape can pull paint off the surface when you remove it from the area you were trying to protect. If you're not good at cutting in with a brush (it does take practice), then consult your paint dealer and ask what brand of tape he or she would suggest you use.

Although most people today use a water-based paint, oil-based paint is still readily available in a wide variety of colors. Should you select an oil-based paint, be aware that cleanup requires turpentine or something equally strong, unlike water-based paint where cleanup requires nothing stronger than soap and water.

Prepare the surface before painting. Oil-base high-gloss paint can magnify any surface flaws such as cracks, nail holes, and a lumpy, bumpy surface. A good washing, spackling compound, painter's putty, and a light sanding can rid your walls of flaws before the new coat of paint is applied.

Because the drying time of today's paint is considerably less than in previous eras, use the paint additive suggested for the type of paint you will be using to slow the drying time down and make the paint easier to work with. Again, don't hesitate to consult your paint dealer. It's their job to guide you through your painting project.

If the ceiling is to be painted along with the rest of the room, paint the ceiling first. Then move to any trim such as crown molding and work your way down, painting door and window trim and ending with the baseboard. Once that has been done, then you can start on the walls.

In real estate location is the thing and in painting good equipment is the thing. If you're going to be using an oil-based paint, you should consider buying a high-quality natural-bristle brush. If you will be working with the more popular water-based paint, then purchase a high-quality synthetic-bristle brush.

If you find that you have to put your paint chore on an extended hold, clean your brush and then wrap it in plastic wrap. It will keep your brush moist and ready to pick up where you left off.

When painting windows, first push the inner sash up and the outer sash down until the two sashes have almost but not quite reversed their position. Start with painting the lower portion of the outer sash before painting the entire inner sash.

After the lower sash is completely dry, move both sashes back to their regular positions, leaving both sashes slightly open until all the surfaces you've painted are dry. Failure to do so can result in windows that are extremely difficult to open.

And finally, what color to choose? If you are totally confused by the virtual mountain of paint colors available and the stack of swatches you've accumulated in the junk drawer of the kitchen, it might help to take a good look at the clothes in your bedroom closet. See what color is the most predominant or the one you like the best because it flatters your coloring (everyone from co-workers to your mother thinks that you look smashing when you wear anything in that particular color). Perhaps you would like a room in that color as well.

When all's said and painted, your home should be a backdrop for your personality and taste in colors.

ABOUT THE AUTHOR

After successfully combining marriage, motherhood, and a business career, **Peg Marberg** returned to school, graduating in 1997 from St. Mary of the Woods College, Terre Haute, Indiana. Peg is a full-time writer. She and her husband are part-time residents of Indiana and Arizona, where they enjoy the company of family, friends, and of course the irrepressible Chaco, aka Pesty.